TERRA NOVA

JESSAHME WREN

For information on other books by this author, visit Jessahme Wren online at https://jessahmewren.com

Paperback ISBN 979-8-9921943-4-0
Hardcover ISBN 979-8-9921943-3-3

Ad astra per aspera
Through hardships to the stars (Latin proverb)

CHAPTER 1

The liquid bubbled in the vial, effervescent and colorful in the natural light from the window. Sev turned the flame down on the burner. She withdrew the pencil from her hair, releasing her blonde tresses, and recorded her findings.

That was the fifth time this solution had boiled slower with sugar added. Perhaps she was on to something, after all.

She thought of her father. Phoenix had always said there was chemistry in cooking. "There's a science to it, little mouse. An order of operations, as it were" he'd told her one sun-drenched afternoon in their little room on Dobani. She smiled to herself, then took up the tongs to remove the hot beaker and empty the contents into the sink.

Sev sat back on her stool and smoothed a hand over her loose hair. She hovered her hand over her holopad, finger touching her father's contact.

◆ ◆ ◆

Phoenix saw his daughter's face in hologram, much younger than she was now. He'd taken that picture maybe three years ago at a local festival. She had been going in circles on a ride, and when she'd come around again, he snapped her photo. Her cheeks had still been full with childhood, but her bright green eyes and infectious smile were the same.

Now she was sixteen. A young woman. But still his little girl.

He answered on the second ring. "Well, hello, sweet mouse. Have you solved all Dobani's mysteries yet with your experimentin'?"

She laughed, soft and light. "Daddy, no," she protested. "But I'm getting close."

"Ah," he said humorously. "I thought you might be." He shut the thick book lying open on the desk in front of him. The library was near closing, and he needed to pack up anyway.

Sev's face brightened on the screen. "How's studying coming? You think you're ready for your test?"

Phoenix considered. "With your stringent quizzes, now who could fail? Help me after dinner tonight?"

She nodded. "Of course, Dad." A brief pause. Then, quieter—"You're going to be an amazing teacher."

Phoenix blushed, as he always did under Sev's praise. He'd entered university almost a year ago. Some days, he could scarcely believe he was in school again. But he loved learning—and more than that, he wanted to impart that love to others.

He muttered his thanks. Sev cleared her throat, breaking the comfortable silence. "What are we having for dinner, anyway?"

He sighed and ran a hand through his hair. "I was thinking skewers. Roast them over the firepit outside. The night is mild enough."

Sev hummed in agreement. "I'll go by the farmer's market and pick up some vegetables. Any preferences?"

"None. I shall leave it to your keen discretion."

She smiled. "Okay, but if it's all purple tubers, there'll be no complaints from you."

Phoenix huffed a laugh. "I shall eat them all and be grateful."

The quiet stretched between them.

Sev hesitated. Phoenix noticed the way her gaze flickered for a second, as if debating something. She shifted, like she wanted to say more.

Instead, she just whispered, "I love you, Dad. I'll see you soon, okay?"

Phoenix's chest tightened. He smiled to himself. "Of course, baby."

The call ended.

On the other end of the line, Phoenix exhaled, slipping his holopad into his bag. The book followed—a tome on interplanetary educational philosophy. He slung the bag over his right shoulder and stood, slower than usual. His muscles protested as he rose, and after steadying himself against the doorframe, he headed out of the library and into the waning sun.

◆ ◆ ◆

The sun slanted over the hood of the transport, casting muted beams of light into the cab. The clouds had dissipated, leaving a blue-gray film over the sky. It was nearing sunset.

Sev had the driver drop her off at the farmer's market. Phoenix had not yet taught her to drive…she had navigated three systems to Terra Firma and back, but she couldn't operate a land transport.

She took her time over the vegetables, milling between the stands and making her purchases. It reminded her of the many times she and Phoenix had stopped, sweat-soaked and stinking from the docks, to pick some produce to cook in their little room.

Satisfied with her selections, she took the bag of vegetables with her back to the transport.

It was dark when the driver dropped her off, the sun having already slipped below the horizon. The windows of their little house by the beach glowed warm and bright. She took her schoolbag and the vegetables she'd purchased and headed up the steppingstone path toward the porch. She opened the front door to muted light and the faint sound of music floating from the living room. Her father was standing at the stove, humming along to the song that played. He hadn't heard her come in.

Sev detoured by her room, dropping her bag on her bed. Little had changed there in as many years…a few more posters decorated the walls, and her bookshelf now sat filled to overflowing. A delicate string of lights hung across her bed, casting her room in a subtle glow. She was so tall now her head nearly brushed them as she walked out toward the kitchen.

She walked up behind her father; he appeared lost in food prep and the old music Sev teased him for listening to. She wrapped her arms around him, resting her head on his shoulder.

Phoenix smiled and dropped the knife he was using to fillet meat for the skewers. He reached for his daughter's hand with his artificial one and gave it a gentle squeeze. "There's the apple of my eye," he said. "I was wondering when you might be in."

She moved to his side, leaned in, and pecked his cheek. "Would have been here sooner if I had my own transport."

He tossed her an apron and took the bag of vegetables, parsing half and giving them back to her. "Soon, mouse. I'm a man of my word." Sev watched as he flexed his left hand. His fingers twitched slightly, and something about the movement bothered her. *Was he in pain?* If he was, he didn't mention it.

Sev pulled a knife from the block and began peeling. "Pearla could teach me, Daddy. You know, if you're too busy."

"Pearla could teach you what?" came a playful voice from the living room. Sev turned, smiling, to see Pearla shrugging off her coat near the front door.

Phoenix approached her, his arms outstretched. Pearla leaned into him, accepting the gentle kiss he offered with a smile and returning it with one of her own. "Sev wants her own transport," Sev heard him murmur. "She thinks I'm taking too long to teach her."

Pearla laughed, withdrawing and approaching Sev. "You're right, of course," she said easily. "Your father is taking his sweet time. You're old enough to drive. More than."

Pearla hugged Sev in greeting, then turned to Phoenix and reached for his hand. She thumbed over the back of it, just a brush of a touch. "But he promised. And I've never seen him break a promise."

Phoenix nodded, pleased. "And I'm not apt to start now. I just want to make sure you're ready, Sev. The roads are dangerous, and I won't be with you always." He winced then, pinching the bridge of his nose. "You girls mind finishing up? I think I'll lie down for a while."

Pearla narrowed her eyes. "Do you feel ok?"

Sev began spearing the vegetables on the skewers piece by piece. "He said he had a headache earlier," she said. She waved dismissively. "He's been studying too hard."

Pearla squeezed his hand reassuringly. "Get some rest. I'll call you when the fire is ready."

◆ ◆ ◆

The meat sizzled and steamed over the open flame of the firepit. Phoenix, Pearla, and Sev each held a skewer over the heat. Pearla had a platter of completed ones beside her, the vegetables charred lightly and meat glistening with fat in the flickering light from the fire.

Sev turned her skewer so the vegetables would cook evenly. "You feel better, Daddy?"

Phoenix smiled at her. "Right as rain, dear heart. Probably like you said. I've been studying too hard."

Pearla nudged his arm, her nose wrinkled. "I think that one is done…your vegetables have gone crispy."

Phoenix frowned, turning his skewer in the firelight. Indeed, one side appeared blackened. "But I like them that way, Pearl."

Sev quirked her mouth; Phoenix often shortened Pearla's name when he was trying to win an argument or otherwise endear her, and it usually worked.

Sev laughed. "Let him go, Pearla. It will be him up sick tonight, not us."

Phoenix patted his belly with his free hand. "Nonsense. I've got a stomach of iron. Mouse, you remember the three-day-old fish I used to pack for my lunch at the docks? And I was sick not one day."

Sev made a face as he pulled the blackened skewer out of the fire finally and lay it on the platter with the rest. She was watching him fondly, and Pearla had a bemused expression on her face.

"Daddy? Would it be ok if we didn't study tonight? It being the weekend tomorrow?"

Phoenix considered. "What have you got in mind, little mouse?"

Sev wavered a bit, looking for the right words. "The holographs. My friends are going tonight, and they asked me along." She looked up at him, seafoam eyes warm in the firelight. "Can I go, Daddy?"

Phoenix worked the fingers of his mechanical hand against his knee, a rhythmic exercise to keep the servos loose. "Just one show," he said. "I want you in your own bed before the tide comes in."

Sev stood and crossed to her father. He met her halfway, swaying a bit as he stood. "Thank you, Daddy," she whispered, throwing her arms around him. "I promise I won't be late."

Phoenix patted her back gently. His touch was warm, familiar and steady, just like it had always been. She felt him exhale, his chest rising and falling against hers.

She was almost as tall as he was now. Not long ago, he had to crouch to hug her. Now, they stood nearly eye to eye.

His arms tightened around her for just a second, and he pressed his face into her hair.

"I know you won't, baby. Have a good time."

Sev pulled away. Her father's tan face had a few more lines etched now, especially when he smiled. Tiny flecks of silver at his temples joined the white patch in his hair. Aside from that, his face was the same one she saw when he tucked her in every night, all those years ago, or when he had dusted her off when she fell off her scooter. That same face loomed over hers whenever she'd been sick, never leaving her side until her fever broke.

"Do you have enough credits?"

Pearla's voice broke from her revelry. She looked and Pearla was patting her pockets, searching for her card. Sev nodded, warmed by the gesture.

"I do. I've got some left from my job at the library." She sat back down in her spot around the fire. "My friends can pick me up right after dinner."

They ate. The night creatures sang as the night grew darker. As soon as they'd finished their meal, Sev went back inside to get ready to go out with her friends, leaving Pearla and Phoenix alone.

The air was chilly. Pearla went inside for a blanket and came back to sit around the dwindling fire with Phoenix. She shared the blanket with him, and he muttered his thanks.

He sat quietly for a long few moments, staring into the embers. Sev's friends pulled up in their transport, and Phoenix watched as Sev walked down the pathway, got in, and drove away.

For a fleeting second, he had the sudden and irrevocable feeling he would never see her again. He blinked, and it was gone.

"She's growing up, Pearla," he said into the fire. "I'm trying to be what she needs, but it's not as easy as it was when she was younger."

Pearla leaned against him, pulling the blanket up to her chin. She rested her cheek on his shoulder, and he wrapped an arm around her. His hand twinged. "Oh Phoenix. You're such a good father, hon. And Sev would tell you right away that you are exactly what she needs."

Phoenix smiled. He turned and pressed a kiss to her mouth, letting his lips linger there. She hummed. "Let's go to bed early," she murmured, and he nodded his agreement.

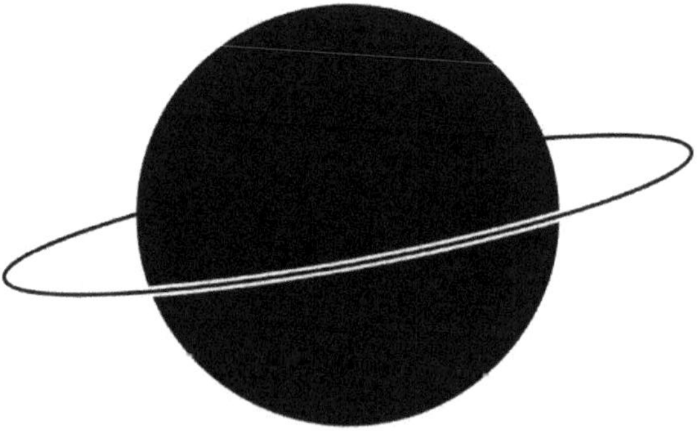

CHAPTER 2

Morning came swiftly, with a beautiful sunrise and low tide. Sev sat at the table in the kitchen, enjoying the warm light from the bay windows and nursing her morning cup of stim brew.

She smiled as she remembered teasing her father for drinking it all those years ago. Now it was an essential start to her day.

"Good morning," Pearla greeted. Sev turned toward her voice and watched as she walked into the kitchen. Pearla pulled her robe tight around her, trembling against the early morning chill. She had her hair up in a messy bun. Sev watched her cross to the pot and pour herself a steaming cup.

Pearla settled across from Sev, blowing over the top of her stim brew before she took a tentative sip. "It's beautiful out there," she remarked as she glanced out the window.

Sev hummed her agreement, wrapping her hands around her cup to leach the warmth there. "I never tire of the view. So serene. So perfect."

Pearla nodded. "Want to go out? We can watch the birds eat their breakfast."

Sev smiled. She gathered up her cup and held her other hand out for Pearla to grab it. "Let's go."

They walked the little boardwalk down to the beach. There were three low wooden chairs there, just outside of Sev's shade. Sev settled in one, and Pearla sat beside her.

For a moment, they said nothing. Sev still had her stim, and she sipped it with her eyes closed against the fragile warmth of the new sun. She buried her feet in the cool sand and listened to the waves, the calls of the birds as they swooped for fish. There wasn't much wind, but the air was still sharp with the overnight chill.

"How were the holographs? What did you see?"

Sev opened her eyes and smiled. "A funny one," she recalled. "Dad would've liked it. Then we went to the diner for dessert."

Pearla brightened. She pulled up one leg beneath her and laid her cup in the sand, momentarily forgotten. "Frosted milk?"

Sev laughed. "Of course. With extra sugar. We stayed for a while and just talked afterward. It was nice."

Pearla nodded. "I'm so glad, Sev. Friends are important. I'm due for tea with mine most any time, now." She quirked her mouth in a small frown. "Friendships get harder as you get older. Too many responsibilities."

Sev looked down at where her feet dug into the sand. The soft grit was up to her ankles now. She thought of the many hours she spent on the beach when they first arrived on Dobani…how she had tottered out into waves without knowing how to swim or even how to stand upright in the water. The shore had welcomed her almost immediately with how natural it felt. But a lot of that had to do with Phoenix. He had always made everything feel like home.

She finally looked up, her thoughts far away.

"Pearla? Can I ask you something?"

Pearla leaned forward, crossing her arms in front of her. "Of course, Sev. What's on your mind?"

Sev licked her lips, considering. "I keep waiting for the right time to ask Dad," she began, "but I can't ever think of the right thing to say, and he's been so tired lately."

Pearla waited for her to continue, the companionable silence between them encouraging Sev to finish her thoughts.

Sev glanced at the waves, unsure of where to begin. "There's a dance at school," Sev said. "A father/daughter dance. A lot of my friends are going with their dads." She blinked away the tears that threatened to fall, unbidden. "I want to ask Dad, but I don't know what he would think of it or what he would say."

Pearla was beaming. She reached over and covered Sev's hand with hers. "Oh Sev. Phoenix would be over the moon; I just know it. You know how he loves you."

Sev nodded, feeling better now that she'd gotten it off her chest. "Oh, I know he does," she agreed. "I have never doubted. I just don't know how to ask…and I don't have anything to wear."

Pearla laughed fondly. "Have you forgotten? I own a store, love. We will find you a beautiful dress!" She clapped her hands excitedly. "Oh, let's go this morning, before your father wakes up. We'll surprise him!"

Sev smiled. She felt so much better now that she had a plan. She and Pearla would get her dress, and then she would ask her dad. He wouldn't be able to say no, then. She could almost see the look on her father's face when he saw her all dressed up…his broad smile, the warmth in his eyes that was there whenever he looked at her, and how proud he would be.

She stood, grabbed her stim cup, and motioned to Pearla. "Ok," she said. "I put myself in your capable hands."

Pearla smiled and picked up her own forgotten stim brew. She followed Sev up the boardwalk and back into the house to get ready.

◆ ◆ ◆

After they had shopped and brunched in Dobani Proper, Sev and Pearla made their way home. Pearla pulled the transport to a stop under the shade of a great palm in the front yard. They divided the packages between them and shouldered their way inside.

It was dark and quiet, very unusual for midday. None of the lights were on, as if Phoenix was still in bed.

It all felt wrong. A jolt of dread went through Sev, and she dropped the packages at the door. Her hand moved slowly, as if through mud, as she reached for the light switch. She couldn't breathe…couldn't think. She flipped it on and flooded the room with light.

Her father was lying on the couch. His eyes were closed, and his arm dangled at an odd angle, almost touching the floor.

She blinked back tears, fighting the panic that threatened to overtake her. She took a few stumbling steps toward the couch. "Daddy?"

Phoenix did not answer. He appeared asleep, but lacked the peace that often came with it. His body was rigid, and there was a fine sheen of sweat coating his face.

Sev exchanged a glance with Pearla; she could see the worry in her eyes that was likely reflected in hers. Pearla dropped her packages as well and they rushed to his side, Pearla kneeling beside him.

She stood frozen as Pearla lightly shook Phoenix's shoulder. "Phoenix… wake up, love." Her voice was calm, but Sev could see the tension in the way her fingers pressed into his skin, the way her breath hitched just slightly.

Pearla placed the back of her hand against his forehead. A sharp inhale. Even without words, Sev knew. He was burning up.

A terrible tightness coiled in Sev's chest. Her own heartbeat pounded in her ears, but she forced herself to stay still, to wait.

"Tell me what's going on," she asked shakily.

Phoenix moaned and tried to move his arm. He only managed it halfway, but high enough to weakly grab Pearla's hand. "Something's wrong," he muttered. His voice was raspy and faint, and he appeared to be in great pain.

Sev reached for her holopad. She had opened an emergency channel before she'd had time to think. She called for help, giving the operator her father's information and what little she knew so far.

Sev shut her eyes. She was back on the skiff, so much younger and terrified out of her mind. Phoenix was there, bleeding out on the floor. She'd called the Terminal for help but had gotten no reply.

She opened her eyes, shaking her head slightly. This was not then…things were different now. Help would come. Her father would be alright.

She dropped to her knees beside Pearla. "Daddy? I need you to tell me what happened. What do you feel?"

Phoenix licked his dry lips. "I tried…call you," he said weakly. "Fingers…wouldn't work. Head is pounding."

Sev smoothed her father's hair back over his fevered head. He was pale, with dewy skin. "Did you lose consciousness, Daddy?"

He nodded. "For a time, mouse. For a time." His eyes rolled, and he seemed to deflate. The grip he had on Pearla's hand lessened. "I'm tired," he said. "Think I'll sleep for a bit."

Pearla reached forward, shaking him lightly. Her eyes were wide with fear. "No Phoenix. Stay with us. Stay awake!" Tears tracked freely down her cheeks, and she was paler than usual.

Sev caressed her father's face. It was hot beneath her fingers. His eyes moved rapidly under closed lids. Fever dreams, most likely. Outside, the alarm of the medical transport sounded plaintive and loud. Relief flooded through her as she heard the transport come to a stop and the medics get out. Things would be ok, now. All would be fine. This was not like on the skiff. Help had come, and her father would be fine.

The medics pushed them both away as they began assessing her father's condition. Sev stood off to the side, relieved now that the medics had arrived, yet worried about Phoenix. The medics exchanged terse words and scanned him with a few instruments. A medic placed a scanner to his temple and read the glyphs on the screen. He looked at the other, a grave set to their mouth. "Vitals are dropping," Sev heard him say, and it chilled her to the bone. The medics finished their scans and loaded him onto the gravbed that sat waiting by the couch. They activated it and rushed him to the transport that sat idling in the front yard.

Sev watched the surreal scene of her father being carted away to the medical transport as if it were a dream. Her father, a constant touchstone of strength and stability, lay stretched out on that gravbed, looking so pale and so fragile. None of it seemed real.

Pearla and Sev followed the medics, getting there just in time to see the doors slam on the transport with Phoenix inside. One medic, a young human male, approached them. "We must go. We're losing time as it is."

Pearla looked at Sev, but Sev's eyes were unfocused and filled with tears. "The medical center?" she asked the medic, and he nodded. Without another word, he ran to the other side of the transport and got in. They were away and down the drive before Pearla could ask anything else.

Pearla walked back over to where Sev stood. Sev was looking down the boardwalk toward the beach. Tears stained her face. "Sev, honey, we have to go. We have to be there for your father."

Sev nodded. She had her arms folded against the wind. She was still trying to process how quickly things had happened…how fast life could change. Her father, the strongest person she knew, was now fighting to survive.

She shook her head. Phoenix needed her. Now was not the time for indulging in such thoughts. "Get the transport," she said to Pearla. "I want to be there when he wakes up."

CHAPTER 3

Med staff had led them to a little waiting area with stale stim brew, disposable cups, and a single viewscreen turned to Dobani news. Sev shifted on the hard chair again, trying to tune out the drone of the newscaster as she discussed the Dobani economy. Pearla was by the window, staring out over the skyline, her arms folded in front of her.

Sev took another sip of the bitter brew and frowned at the taste. Her father, who she considered a stim brew connoisseur, would've had a word or two to say about this cup, for sure. She smiled, but it quickly vanished under the realization of why she was there.

The last time she'd been at the medical center, she had been with her father. They'd both been so happy. It was when the doctors had fitted Phoenix with his new arm. They'd walked out of the medical center and into the rest of their lives, so ripe with promise and possibility.

She stood, tossed her cup in the nearby trash receptacle and reached for a fresh one. She poured the stim brew all the way to the top and carefully walked toward where Pearla stood at the window. Sev placed a hand on her arm, making sure not to startle her. She handed Pearla the cup with a quirk of her mouth.

Pearla smiled. "I suppose I will. Something's got to keep me going."

Sev made a face. "It's not pleasant, but it gets the job done. Stuff is stronger than a Dobani Water Walker."

It made Pearla laugh. She sipped the steaming cup, then grimaced. "You weren't lying about it being strong."

Sev smiled softly. "You're strong too, Pearla. We both are." She put a hand on Pearla's shoulder, letting it linger there. "We have to be strong for Dad."

Pearla put her cup down and hugged her, resting her head on her shoulder. "Yes," she said tearfully. "I promise I'm trying. It's just—"

She looked up and saw the doctor walk slowly into the room. He was holding a holopad and looked hesitant to interrupt.

"Are you with Mr. Phoenix?"

Pearla withdrew, and she and Sev turned toward the doctor. "We both are," Sev said.

"Who should I speak to concerning his care?" the doctor asked.

Sev stepped forward. "Whatever you have to say, you can say to both of us."

The doctor swallowed. He glanced down at his holopad. "Perhaps we should sit," the doctor suggested. He led them both to the sitting area where Sev had spent most of her day. The viewscreen was still blaring; a jaunty jingle advertising toothpaste filled the silence between them.

"What's going on?" Sev asked. "How's my dad? Can we see him?"

The doctor pressed his lips together. "Your father is very sick. I'm afraid all we can do for him is keep him comfortable until we find out what's going on."

Pearla leaned forward. "You mean you don't know? Why don't you know?" She shook her head, visibly agitated. "I don't understand."

"Can we see him?" Sev repeated, her voice edged with tension.

The doctor nodded. "Please, follow me."

Sev and Pearla followed the doctor down the bright and winding hallways. Beeps and whirs of various machinery and scanners punctuated the air as they passed. There were patients in rooms on either side of them, but Sev kept her eyes fixed ahead. Although outwardly she appeared calm, inside she was experiencing a tumult of emotions. She was excited to see her father, but also terrified of how she might find him. It was a noxious mix.

The doctor led them to an overly bright area with a large glass room in the middle. Inside, under a host of wires and tubes, was her father.

"Drek," she whispered. "Oh, Daddy." Sev's eyes filled with tears. She'd seen her father spore-sick on Terra Firma…she'd seen him injured and bleeding. She had never seen him like this.

"You can go in and see him…touch him. He can probably hear you, but he can't reply," the doctor said.

Pearla walked up to one of the glass walls and placed her hands against it. She looked exhausted to Sev, physically and emotionally spent. "What's his prognosis?" Pearla asked quietly. "What have we got to do to get him well?"

The doctor looked down before responding. "His prognosis is uncertain," he said tersely. "He has an infection. That's all we know. We need more information, but we have reached the ceiling of our knowledge."

Sev stepped forward, her body rigid. "Then we'll take him somewhere else," she resolved. "To Ocarro. They're famous for their advancements in medicine, aren't they? In figuring out hard to solve cases? I learned about them in school. They'll know what to do."

The doctor nodded. "If that's what you wish, miss. Keep in mind, though, that not even Ocarro might help him. And he might not survive the transport."

Pearla looked at Sev. "It's an awfully long way, Sev," Pearla said. "Are we sure we should risk it?"

Sev thought for a moment. They could do nothing, and her father would die right here on Dobani. Or they could risk it on the off chance that he might live.

She bit back tears, her jaw clenched. He would do it for her.

"Do it," Sev said. "In the meantime, I want to see my dad."

She did not wait for permission. She opened the door to the glass room and navigated the various machines there, Pearla following close behind. They found Phoenix lying on the bed. The Dobani medics had taped his eyes shut. An inflatable bulb counted his breaths, inflating and deflating every few seconds with a decompressing puff of air. He was not wearing his arm. The medical staff had dressed him in the pale blue shirt and pants that every medical center patient wore. He was still and appeared asleep. Sev kneeled beside him and held his remaining hand.

"Daddy? It's me. It's Sev." She clutched his hand as if she could imbue life into him with sheer will alone. She looked at his face for any reaction, but she did not see any. His hair stood spiked over his forehead, the white patch almost iridescent in the unnatural light.

"Pearla's here too, Daddy. We love you." She let her thumb brush over the back of his hand. His skin was dry and feverish. "We're going to get you somewhere they can help you. Maybe Ocarro. I don't know yet. But I'll let you know as soon as I do."

Pearla reached out and brushed his hair back from his forehead. "We'll be here, Phoenix. For as long as you need us."

Sev locked eyes with Pearla and gave her a brief nod. She leaned forward and pressed a kiss to her father's feverish cheek. She lingered there, and her eyes slipped closed. *Please, please Daddy,* she silently pleaded before finally withdrawing to look down on him.

He remained silent and unresponsive, his usual tan skin pale against the white pillow.

Sev gave his hand a parting squeeze, released him, and left Pearla at his bedside.

She'd had enough of no answers and evasive prognoses. They'd made their home on Dobani, but Sev knew better than anyone that every planet had limitations. It was time to move on into the Black. She didn't know what answers Ocarro might hold, but it was worth a try.

Sev walked straight to the medic station, intent on moving things along and finally getting her father the treatment he deserved.

CHAPTER 4

They moved him on a Saturday. Sev spent the morning pacing in front of the glass box, looking in on her father as they prepared him for transport. Usually, her Phoenix would read the holonews on Saturday morning, the reading glasses he only recently needed perched on the end of his nose. She could almost hear the faint rustle of the holopages, the clink of the cup from her father setting it back in its saucer. She would come out of the kitchen, and he would look at her over his glasses, smile, and inquire about her plans for the day.

Sev would give anything now to have him back at home and well again. Those familiar routines seemed so precious, in retrospect. So mundane, yet so important.

She watched Pearla through the glass. Pearla had moved only to use the facilities. What little she slept and ate, she did at Phoenix's bedside, and at Sev's urging.

Sev had seen Phoenix incapacitated…she'd seen him through the worst of it on Terra Firma. Pearla only new Phoenix as strong, charming, and kind. She'd never seen him weakened, and it was breaking her.

The doctor approached Sev, and his presence pulled her from her thoughts. "We're almost ready to move your father," he said. "This is the riskiest part of the transport, when we disconnect the machines." He followed

Sev's line of vision through the glass walls. "I'm sorry we couldn't do more for him here." He patted Sev's arm. "I wish you all the best, though."

Sev watched him walk away, then looked back toward Phoenix's bed. A crowd of medics were flitting around her father, so many that she could no longer see him. Pearla was standing in the corner, her hand to her mouth.

Sev pushed through the glass door and walked toward him. She could only get so far before the bodies and machines got in the way. Sev slipped her hand through the chaos, patting her father on the arm. She sent him all the strength she could muster, silently willing him to hold on, to be strong through the transfer.

She stepped back, retreating to the corner to watch with Pearla. Pearla had one hand over her stomach, and the other still hovered near her face. Sev wrapped an arm around her, and she laid her head on her shoulder.

In one quick movement, the medics got him on the gravbed. Alarms blared…sensors beeped. They hurried to reconnect the various tubes and hoses, the mechanical devices that were keeping him alive. With the medics cleared, Sev could see him again. His face appeared drawn and bereft of color. He no longer looked asleep. He looked very far away.

There was a shrill tone, and the readouts on the scanners went suddenly haywire. The medics studied the glyphs, barking orders while others wielded various phials and infusions. The doctor rushed in, assessing the situation. "You'll have to leave," he said to them. "If we're to get him to the transport alive, it has to be now."

Sev looked at Pearla; she appeared stricken, her usually bright eyes hollow and dull. "Someone has to be with him," Pearla muttered. "He can't go to Ocarro alone."

Sev considered. If Phoenix died in transit, she didn't want Pearla there. Sev knew death intimately…had faced it as a young child. Del died right in front of her. Phoenix almost did. Her mother when she was just a babe, though she couldn't remember it.

"I'll go with him," Sev told her. "The medical center will arrange a transport for you. You'll be right behind us."

Pearla hugged her. "Thank you, love," she whispered. She patted her back. "Your father raised an amazing daughter. You know how proud he is."

Tears welled in her eyes. Sev knew. *The apple of his eye*, he had said. His little mouse. If Phoenix didn't make it—

She shook her head, pushing the thought away. He would make it. He had to.

"Phoenix is stable for now," the doctor said. "It's time to go. Who will go with him?"

Pearla stepped up. "His daughter. I'll go on after." She gave her a gentle smile. "Good luck to the both of you," Pearla said to her. "May Drek be with you."

Sev nodded. "Drek be with us all," she murmured. "You sure you will be ok?"

Pearla nodded. "I'll be on right after, like you said." She hugged Sev fiercely. "I love you," she whispered. "You take care of your father until I can get there, ok?"

Sev smiled, hugging her back. "I will Pearla. Try not to worry."

Pearla laughed half-heartedly. "Oh, I will worry. But that's ok too."

Sev turned, and the gravbed floated by her, medics in tow. She waved goodbye to Pearla and jogged to catch up with it until she had pulled even with her father. She reached for his hand.

"I'm here, Daddy. I'm always going to be here." She squeezed, imagining him squeezing back. "We're going to Ocarro. Have you ever been there? When you wake up, you can tell me if you were. And you'll probably have a story about it, too."

A finger on his left hand twitched, and it encouraged her. "Good, Daddy. Stay with me. Just like that."

Up ahead, the medical center hallway opened to the warm Dobani sun. She could see it streaming through the open double doors. Outside, a medical transport was waiting to take them to the landing pad.

Ocarro was a desolate, snowy planet, or so her schoolbooks had told her. Sev had never seen snow. She wished more than anything that her father was awake, so he could see it too. She wondered briefly how it would feel…would it be silken or gritty? How would it be to walk in it, to have it fall all around her?

Sev stood back and let the medics get her father situated. When they had locked the gravbed into place, and the containment hood that separated her from her father was a clear but present barrier between them, Sev sat on the little bench in the back of the transport. With the hood activated, she could not hold his hand. She pressed her fingers against the forcefield, watching the pressure make little halos at the contact. Her father lay beneath. He no longer needed the ventilation equipment now, with the containment hood. He breathed seemingly on his own, though Sev knew different. She watched the rise and fall of his chest, each breath stoking the embers of hope that dwelled within her.

The transport pulled away, sirens blazing, as she and Phoenix made their way to the landing pad.

CHAPTER 5

They were in the Black. Phoenix could hear the hum of the engines, could feel the vibration of the thrusters through the thin-paneled walls of the ship. Only the skiff never felt like this…the skiff was both loud and quiet, near silent in the depths of space and as creaky as an old joint upon reentry.

No, this was not the skiff. His Sev wasn't at the navigation screen, for one. And—

He tried to move, to raise his head. It wouldn't budge. Fear ratcheted through him. *Was he restrained?* Phoenix tried his legs, his arms. They were heavy as stone. Then he realized his prosthetic was gone. He'd grown so used to it these past years that its absence was palpable.

He heard something else…the high-pitched whine of a forcefield somewhere nearby.

With a great deal of effort, Phoenix opened his eyes. He saw the bluish hue of a forcefield shimmering right above his face. And past that, the top of a transport. He was in the Black, after all.

"Daddy?"

He tried to turn his head, to follow her voice, but he could not. Sev hovered over him, her skin pale through the pallor of the forcefield separating them. She called to him again, her voice muffled through the invisible barrier. Sev put her hands against the clear hood, her fingers spread. Phoenix blinked at her, willing her closer. Her hair hung down around her face. It pooled against the surface of the forcefield. In his mind, he tried to touch it. He tried to reach her hands, to press his against hers.

A single tear rolled down onto his pillow when he realized he could not.

Mouse? Can you hear me? What's happening? Why can't I move?

For the first time since waking, he truly saw her—her eyes searching his face, her expression tight with something unspoken. His gaze softened.

"You're going to be ok Daddy," she gritted out. "I'm not going to let you die. Do you understand me? We've been through too much to let this beat us."

It frightened Phoenix. *Die? Was he sick? Sev looked so stricken. Was it because of him?*

A sudden wave of exhaustion washed over him. He closed his eyes and struggled to open them again. He could hear Sev pleading with him from so far away. "Don't fall asleep Daddy. Stay with me."

Phoenix tried to reply, to give her some sort of sign. *"I love you, mouse,"* he wanted to say, but he was so tired. It was the last thought he had before darkness claimed him.

◆ ◆ ◆

They were two standard hours out from Ocarro, or so the transport operator had said. The medical center had arranged passage for her on a transport to take her off Dobani. From her calculations, she wasn't too far behind Phoenix and Sev.

She was afraid, though she tried not to show it. Pearla was afraid for Phoenix, of course, but deep down, she also feared the unknown that presented itself to her now with every galactic mile she traversed.

Aside from Merren, Pearla had never been off Dobani.

She had not told Phoenix this…that she had limited experience traveling between planets. Pearla wondered how he would react, knowing she was so inexperienced compared to him. She had just never had the need. She was born on Dobani, raised there, and had made her livelihood there. All the travel she had done for work was in-world. Her trip to Merren had been her first time off

24

Dobani. When she had resolved to go all those years ago to bring Sev home, she'd been terrified, though she hid it well. Now, years later, she was so happy she had made the trip.

Pearla often sat in awe when Phoenix regaled her with tales of his travels. He was so worldly, so knowledgeable of places beyond what she could see. Even Sev, in her early life, had traveled extensively. She felt well and truly out of place in the light of their experiences.

She might've been out of her depth alongside them, but she was committed to making it to Ocarro and being there for them both. Pearla might not have logged the miles, but she had the heart. She had determination. That had to count for something.

So far, the trip had been no different from when she'd taken transports to market on the other side of Dobani, and she was relieved. She suffered a little nausea, but her stomach had been ill at ease for a while now. Pearla brushed it off as stress or from a tepid cup of tea and had thought nothing of it. She focused on keeping her breathing even and not moving too much, else it became worse.

Yes, this trip was something entirely other…something unexpected, but so was meeting Phoenix, and she was so glad she had.

Her thoughts turned to him. She closed her eyes and reached out over the miles that separated them. It no longer seemed so foreign now to go to Ocarro. Sev would be there, after all, and she took comfort in that. The young woman she had met as a little girl…the young woman who had slowly become one of her dearest friends. As for Phoenix, she would follow him anywhere, so visiting this new planet was no great thing.

The transport suddenly shook, dropping out quickly and then pulling up again. The lights in the cabin blinked, and outside her window, a smear of stars glowed against a black canvas, hazy and nondescript. Pearla could feel her seat vibrating; even the paneled walls of the cabin shook. Her stomach protested the abrupt movement, and bile rose in her throat. She covered her hand with her mouth, feeling quite ill.

The comm buzzed to life. "Ma'am, we're in a solar storm right now. Better buckle up. Things could get bumpy."

She blindly reached for the safety restraints, her hand shaking a bit. After she had strapped in, she pressed the button on the panel next to her. "How long until we get there?" she asked weakly, stomach still churning against the sudden turbulence.

The speaker beeped once, and it took a moment for the operator to answer. "'Nother hour and a half," he said tensely. "Maybe longer with this storm."

She muttered her thanks. Her stomach had eased for now, despite the transport now shaking around her. Pearla sat back against the seat and thought of Drek, a deity Phoenix often spoke to in times of trouble. She remembered once that Phoenix said Drek didn't care where you started or where you came from, only that you believed. She wondered if Drek would hear her now, unknown to her as she was. Dobani was not a world of deities, but Pearla kept an open mind and an open heart, and from what she had heard of religion, that was more than enough.

Pearla lowered her head. If there was anything out there, Drek or otherwise, she would ask them for their favor on this trip and in the days to come.

CHAPTER 6

Sev saw it in the view pane of the transport…a glowing white globe in the distance, growing larger by the moment.

It was Ocarro. The unceasing snow on the surface of the planet left it pale from space, a large white circle gleaming in the Black.

Sev leaned over the containment hood, looking at her father beneath. "We're almost there, Daddy," she whispered to him. "We're almost there."

His eyes were closed; he had not regained consciousness since he had opened his eyes right after they left Dobani. But if he did it once, he could do it again, she reasoned, so she kept talking to him, encouraging him to hang on.

"Daddy? Have you ever seen the snow?" Sev considered. "I bet you have. You've been everywhere." She looked down at him, tears welling in her eyes. "I wish we were visiting Ocarro for different reasons," she mused. "Like when you would take me on holiday after I brought home good grades, and we would tour whatever city we were in like it was our first time on Dobani." She wiped away a stray tear, remembering. "Or the time when you let me pick the destination, and I chose a place on the map that was known for its mud baths, all because I liked the name." She smiled at the memory. "*Bubble Lake*. You remember that, Daddy?"

Sev looked down at Phoenix's still face. His eyes moved rhythmically beneath tight lids. The faint lines around his eyes were only there when he smiled, so he looked younger in sleep. He looked vulnerable…not the strong man she knew so well.

She looked at the glyphs on the readout. The medics had told her he was stable, but she still scrutinized the data as if she could understand what it meant. Below, Phoenix's lids flickered as if he was trying to wake up. The slight movement caught her attention immediately.

"That's it, Daddy. I know you're in there. I know you can hear me." She smiled and placed her hand against the forcefield. "Wake up so you can tease me about *Bubble Lake*. About the mud we couldn't get out of our clothes."

His eyelashes fluttered, and Sev held her breath. She sent a silent prayer out into the universe…for her father, for the staff on Ocarro that was waiting to care for him. Talking to him was working…she could feel it.

Outside the view pane, Ocarro grew larger and more detailed. Sev could see the jagged lines of mountain ranges…the deep blue spots of lakes, the squiggly outline of rivers. The transport would enter atmosphere soon. She reached for the restraints and buckled herself in. *Almost there*, she thought to herself. It filled her with hope and wonder, both.

◆ ◆ ◆

The transport rumbled and shook. Phoenix knew they were about to land; he'd been in the Black most of his life, and the way gravity dropped out right before breaking atmosphere was unmistakable. Even lying on his back, as odd as that was, it made the pit of his stomach lurch.

He tried to move his hand, tried to signal Sev. *I'm here, mouse. I can hear you*, he yearned to say. Phoenix focused all his will on moving; he concentrated so hard that sweat beaded his forehead. After a few moments, he could feel the tip of his finger twitch.

It was something, at least, he tried to reassure himself. He could move…it just took effort. He applied the same effort to opening his eyes. When it worked, the feeling of joy nearly took his breath.

He looked around as best he could without moving his head. Sev was near; he knew that, even though he could not see her. The inside of the transport was very utilitarian. Equipment hung from the roof above him, scanners and machines he was not familiar with. He let his eyes shut for a moment, half-afraid that he wouldn't be able to open them again.

He felt the transport dip, then right itself. Phoenix could hear the thrusters engage, feel the drag of the engine as it stuttered to a stop. He opened his eyes. Above him, cables from the various unfamiliar scanners swung wildly. The entire transport shook, rattling his bones and awaking an acute pain in his head. He remembered now, lying on the couch in his house on Dobani with a splitting headache. It seemed so long ago.

With a rough touchdown, the transport settled on the surface of the planet.

Sev hovered over the forcefield, her face in his view. Her eyes were puffy and red, as if she hadn't slept, but the love there was unmistakable. She had her hands spread over the containment field as if she were trying to connect with him. "We're here Daddy. We made it to Ocarro." Her voice was thick with some unnamed emotion and trembled with unspent tears.

Phoenix could scarcely believe he heard her right. *Ocarro?* His mind raced with possibilities. *Ocarro was known for its medicine. Was he so sick he had to come here?*

Before he had time to consider, he heard the gravbed hiss and disengage. The transport hatch opened with a puff of steam and snow and people dressed in cold-weather uniforms began activating the anti-grav sensors on his capsule. He watched as Sev stood back, letting them work, and he slowly started moving.

The transport opened to a blinding white sky…a beautiful sky. There were people on either side of him; grim faces with unblinking black eyes looked down on him from fur-lined hoods. He could hear Sev as she struggled to keep up, as she asked about him, her voice nearly lost on the wind that swept across the frozen plain.

Foreign hands covered the forcefield. Disembodied voices floated above him, clipped and efficient, but he couldn't make out what they were saying. Above him, snow swirled in pretty patterns against the blank canvas of daylight. He hadn't seen snow since he was a boy, and it momentarily dazzled him. Ahead, cutting a jagged line into the sky, Phoenix saw snowcapped mountains wreathed in clouds, and beyond, a slice of deep blue.

Where are they taking me? Where is Pearla? He broadcasted these frantic questions to anyone who could hear him, though he knew they couldn't. He tried concentrating on moving again, but he was too tired. The pain in his head worsened, blurring his awareness. His unanswered questions drifted away, replaced by his struggle to stay awake.

◆ ◆ ◆

Sev shook against the cold, ill-equipped for the climate. She'd had no time to grab a coat before leaving, and even that might not have been enough. A female medic broke off from the ensemble that was guiding her father into the medical center and wrapped her in a foil insulator. She smiled, muttering thanks as they walked behind her father's medical pod and into the imposing building.

The medical center's main building took her breath. She stopped inside the threshold, momentarily stunned.

There were rows of green plants on either side of the central walkway. The leaves glistened with dew, and nested inside each one was a single glowing flower. The ceiling stretched on for hundreds of feet, its glass roof letting in the muted daylight. Ocarri workers stood among the rows of plants with holopads, test tubes, and various other instruments. They wore masks and protective suits as they fussed over the curious vegetation.

The female medic who had given her the insulator gestured to the other Ocarri. "Our gardens are part of what we do here on Ocarro," she said. "The soil here has healing properties…most of the plant life has a medicinal use."

They walked on, trying to catch up to Phoenix and the others. The gardens reminded Sev of when she was younger, and Phoenix had built her a little garden behind their house on Dobani. She'd spent countless hours fussing over and caring for each plant.

Sev turned to her, pointing to the plants by her feet. "What flowers are those? They glow."

The medic laughed. "Those are the Lumiers," she said. "Their pollen has curative properties. Very important to healing here."

Sev nodded. It was warm inside the medical center, but she kept the insulator around her shoulders. The wrap was comforting; it reminded her of when she and Phoenix would walk along the beach in the off season, and he would take his coat off and drape it around her, sheltering her from the chilly Dobani winds.

She blinked tears from her eyes, grounding herself. Phoenix needed her. Pearla needed her. She could lose herself in her memories later.

Up ahead, her father disappeared around a corner. When she and the medic finally caught up to him, there were medical personnel everywhere. A tall Ocarri woman holding a holopad stopped them in the hall. She had pale skin and mirrored black eyes, the same as all Ocarri. Her hair was white and done up in a bun.

"We're getting your father settled," she said matter-of-factly. "We have a comfortable waiting area for you while we assess his condition."

Sev balked. She stepped forward, wanting to brush past her, to charge into her father's room and see him for herself.

She didn't. Deep down, she knew this was best, albeit hard to accept.

The woman smiled at her, probably sensing her discomfort. "Don't worry, dear. Your father is in expert hands. Ocarri medicine is the best in the galaxy." She led them into a cozy sitting room with a nutrition station, dim lighting, and paintings on the wall. The medic who had walked with her into the medical center patted her on the shoulder, then joined the older woman with the clipboard where she stood in the doorway.

Sev looked at them both. "You'll let me know something soon, right?" She fidgeted lightly, looking down at her hands. "My father is all I have. Please do what you can," she said, her voice thick with emotion.

The woman nodded, and the two of them left her in the waiting room.

Sev looked around. The room was pleasant on the surface; the Ocarri had obviously designed it to project a facsimile of comfort, to put people at ease. Plush couches and chairs littered the room in soft finishes. Squat tables with lamps shone with a welcoming glow. The nutrition station was well stocked…Sev had never seen so many choices in one place. There was a hydration machine in the corner serving up warm beverages. Exotic, glowing plants stood throughout.

She'd never felt more alone.

Her lower lip quivered before she realized it. All the emotions, the adrenaline of the last dozen hours, had taken their toll. She felt decimated…raw with unexpressed grief. She blinked and felt a tear escape her lashes. Sev furiously swiped at it as it tracked its way down her cheek.

There was a chrono on the wall, its large hands relentless and foreboding. With every moment that passed, her father slipped farther and farther away from her.

Sev drew her knees up in the plush chair, pulled the stiff insulator closer around her, and fell into a fitful sleep.

CHAPTER 7

Soren held his cup under the stim dispenser and watched the hot, brown liquid fill the cup almost to the rim. He withdrew, blew on the steam, and took a careful sip. The stim brew warmed him. He had pulled a double and had been awake for twenty-four solar hours.

He took his cup to his desk and looked over his case notes. The consultation on the new patient admission was taking place in the conference room soon, so he packed up his holopad and hurried out the door, stim brew in hand.

Soren looked down at his chrono. He was five minutes late.

With a wince, he turned the knob on the conference room door, and it opened with an earsplitting groan.

The lead doctor stopped talking, turned, and looked pointedly at Soren.

"Good of you to join us, young man."

Soren gave him a half smile, slightly embarrassed. "I apologize for my tardiness. Time must've gotten away from me."

The lead doctor smirked, eyeing his cup. "I see you had time for stim, though. Did you also have time to review the notes on the new intake?"

Soren's face reddened. His hair, as unruly as usual, fell into his eyes, and he swept his hand across his forehead, clearing his vision.

"Phoenix, 39-year-old human male, amputee on the right side, suffering from unknown systemic failure," he recited. He might've been late, but he wasn't negligent. There were four other doctors sitting around the conference table, and the one nearest him gave him an approving nod. Soren acknowledged him; he had mentored him through school and was a good doctor and a kind man. Soren cleared his throat. "Are the scans back?"

The lead doctor steepled his fingers and leaned slightly over his holopad. "They are, and they're grim. It's a viral infection. Widespread."

Another doctor raised his eyebrows. "Cause?"

The doctor lowered the lights in the room with a wave of his hand and activated his holopad. The image of a ghostly transparent green planet flickered to life and hovered there in the middle of the conference table.

Everyone grew quiet, deathly still. The tension in the air was tremulous…a palpable thing.

"Spores," the doctor said, pointing to the hologram. "From this planet. He must've been injured there, or he breathed them in. Either way, they remained dormant in his bloodstream for years, steadily poisoning him."

The doctor nearest Soren made a shocked sort of sound. "Is that…is that Terra Firma?"

Soren narrowed his eyes. The lead doctor did not answer. The hologram shone in the low light of the room, staticky and glowing, its pallor haunting and seemingly innocuous as it spun on its invisible axis. He raised the lights and deactivated the holopad. Terra Firma disappeared.

"Forbidden," another doctor whispered, stricken with horror. Soren looked at him. He was middle-aged, with a wispy mustache that nearly covered his mouth.

"Yes, forbidden," the lead doctor affirmed.

Soren frowned. "What do you mean, sir, by 'forbidden'?"

The doctor grunted. He looked at Soren with barely restrained annoyance. "No one can go there. Not since the accident."

It got Soren's attention. "Accident?"

The doctor on the end, a tall man with a narrow face and pale Ocarri skin, tapped the edge of the table.

"A research crew traveled there about a year ago. Over one hundred scientists, some of them Ocarri." He looked at Soren, his mouth a grim line. "They were never heard from again."

Soren swallowed, his throat feeling tight. He looked around at the other doctors. Some of them had their heads lowered in deference.

"Rescue efforts proved useless and only resulted in more disappearances," the doctor continued. "The Council of Planets met and decided a galaxy-wide ban was in order. No travel to Terra Firma for any reason under penalty of law."

Soren blew out a breath. His quick mind was alight with possibilities…he just had to decide how he wanted to proceed with such a prickly audience.

"If it is viral," he began carefully, "we could make a serum." His black eyes widened, alight with excitement. "We could cure him."

The lead doctor shook his head. "There can be no serum, Soren," he said. "Terra Firma is forbidden. We would need spores. It's impossible."

"Lumiers is what is needed," the mustached doctor interrupted. The remaining doctors nodded and mumbled their agreement.

"Lumiers, yes," the tall doctor said. The lead doctor wrote some notes on his holopad. "That will keep him comfortable."

It struck Soren deeply. That's what they'd said about his mother…that the Lumiers would keep her comfortable. That she would get better on her own.

But she didn't. And after the Lumiers, she never woke up again.

He shook his head, shaking off the memory. "Gentleman," he began, surprised at the strength in his voice. "If there were spore samples in the main laboratory…then we could make the serum without risk. And this man could live again."

The lead doctor pounded the table, startling the kind older doctor to his left. "There are no samples, boy. They were all destroyed after the accident." He shook his head. "You and your wild ideas are a detriment to this medical center…to what we do here."

"Young Soren means well," the kind old doctor intoned. The other doctors looked at him curiously. His peers respected him, and he always commanded an audience. "If we don't look beyond the obvious, how can we treat the impossible?"

Soren couldn't suppress a smile.

The lead doctor inclined his head. "Sometimes, old friend, the impossible is just too insurmountable."

They adjourned the meeting. Soren sat for a moment in the empty conference room, processing what had just happened. He had gone into medicine to save lives…to give people their lives back after illness. He wanted to help people. To Soren, it seemed he rarely got to do that here, and every time he got close to a breakthrough, he hit a brick wall of Ocarri rules and regulations.

Days like these, he wondered to himself why he had chosen medicine at all.

Soren took his stim brew, gone cold now, and gathered up his holopad. He left, feeling more defeated and more tired than ever.

Soren tossed the cold stim brew in the first trash receptacle he passed. He'd get more on the way, he resolved. After all, he needed the energy boost if he was going to get through the next shift.

Soren walked down the hall, lost in thought. The waiting room was just up ahead, its large windows to the corridor beckoning him. The hydration station was within…he could refresh his stim there.

He slowed down as he approached. There was someone already inside.

A young woman sat curled up in a chair. She had a stiff foil insulator wrapped around her and her knees drawn up to her chest. Some of her hair had come free from her ponytail, and it hung loose around her face. It was light, so she was not Ocarri. She was someone from off-world, then, probably waiting on news from a relative.

He sighed. She looked uncomfortable despite her sleep. Curled up under the insulator, she looked small. He felt a twinge of empathy for her. He remembered sleeping in a similar room waiting for news of his mother…news that rarely came, or that was soul-crushing when it did. It was years ago, but the pain was fresh.

Soren looked down at his cold cup and warred with himself. If he opened the door, it would likely disturb her. But maybe if he was quiet…

He took a breath and opened the door.

Blessedly, it made no noise. He smiled in relief, pleased with himself for his stealth. He approached the hydration station carefully. Soren took a quick look over his shoulder. The woman still slept.

Then the hydrator made an obnoxious churning noise as it dispensed his brew, and Soren cringed at how loud it was in the small space. Behind him, he heard her stir.

"Excuse me," he heard her say sleepily, "but are you a medic here?"

Soren turned around. He jammed his hands in his pockets, then took them out again, trying to look professional. He felt terrible for waking her up. The least he could do was be helpful.

She had the loveliest green eyes he'd ever seen.

Soren blinked. They were the color of the ground when not touched by ice and snow…moss-covered and alive. Right now, they were large and questioning.

He smiled nervously. "Yes," he said, clearing his throat. "I'm a medic." He remembered himself and stepped forward to offer his hand. She took it. "I'm Soren. How may I help you?"

The woman gave him a tired smile. "I'm Sev. My dad is here. I was waiting for news, but no one ever came back. You're the first medic I've seen."

Soren brightened. Maybe he could help her, he thought. "Well, what's your dad's name? I can find out something for you."

Sev smiled fondly. "His name is Phoenix. Can you tell me how he's doing?"

Dread settled in his gut. He swallowed. "Well, I'm just a first-year medic," he waffled. "But the other doctors can fill you in. I'll send them."

Sev looked crestfallen. The light in her beautiful green eyes dimmed a bit with disappointment. Then she studied him sharply. "I don't believe you," she finally said.

He was caught out. He swallowed thickly, trying to think. "It's true, I'm just first-year," he said, desperately trying to save his deception with a bit of truth.

"But you know something about my dad."

Her voice was harder this time. It was not a question, and Soren realized this woman was not the frail and grieving family member he'd taken her for. She was strong…used to getting her way.

"Sev? Sweetheart? Any news?"

They both turned toward the voice. A slight woman with bright blue hair stood in the doorway. Sev approached her, letting the foil insulator drop to the floor, and opened her arms to her.

"Pearla," she said. "I'm so glad you're here." Sev hugged her fiercely, her eyes closed. Soren looked away, feeling like he was intruding.

He walked toward the door, looking back at the two women as they embraced. He was so happy Sev was not alone anymore. That she he had someone to wait with. "I'll let you visit with your mom. It was nice to meet you, Sev."

Sev withdrew. A shadow passed over her face, and she looked at him with those piercing green eyes…as green as the fields he'd only read about in books. "My mom died a long time ago," she said. "Not long after I was born."

It hit Soren like a brick. Her mother was dead…and soon her father would be too. Sev would be an orphan. Somehow, it felt like his fault.

The tears came unbidden, but he blinked them away. His throat grew thick, and he swallowed around the lump there. "Well, I'm sorry to have interrupted," he muttered. He glanced at the woman Sev had called Pearla. Her expression was kind, but aggrieved. As for Sev, he could scarcely look at her.

Soren made a hasty departure. The grief in that room brought up too many memories for him. He needed to get to his office. He needed time to think.

CHAPTER 8

They finally let them see him.

He looked thin lying there in that enormous bed. The Ocarri had taken his tunic, and he lay shirtless and pale against the white sheets. Different sensors dotted his usual tan skin. His hair was slicked back, and a halo of sensors circled his head.

His lips sealed against a heavy mask. Sev watched the attached hose as it vibrated with artificial breath. She looked at her father's closed eyes, willing him to wake up.

Pearla sat in a chair beside Phoenix, holding his hand. She talked to him quietly, but Sev couldn't hear what she was saying.

Sev looked on, her eyes soft. Pearla was a kind woman…a strong woman. She loved her father and her.

She was not taking this well.

Sev had known loss in her brief life. She had experienced heartbreak and loneliness. Those collective experiences had formed a callous over her heart. It made things like this—impossible things—just a little easier to handle.

Pearla had no such defense, and Sev worried for her.

The door to Phoenix's room opened, shaking her from her thoughts. A team of doctors walked in, and Pearla stood, her eyes hopeful. Sev crossed to join her.

The doctor in front cleared his throat. He was holding a holopad. "We've reviewed your father's case," he told Sev. "He is sick from exposure to spores. Spores on Terra Firma."

Sev went cold. That night in the miner's tent on Terra Firma all those years ago came rushing back. How sick he'd been. How much he'd coughed. She'd tried to help, but had it been enough?

"My father hasn't been on Terra Firma for years," Sev said. "There must be some mistake."

The young medic she'd met earlier, Soren, stepped forward. "There's no mistake, Sev. Spores from Terra Firma are making your father sick. They remained dormant all these years, but they were slowly poisoning him."

A single tear slipped down her cheek. She looked into the medic's mirrored black eyes. They appeared warm, despite their absence of color.

"You knew this earlier? And you didn't say?" She looked hurt…betrayed. A thread of anger creased her brow. "Answer me."

Soren swallowed. "I'm sorry," he whispered.

A tear ran down her cheek. Terra Firma was a dark blot on their shared history…a terrifying place she'd left in the past. She thought they'd beat it. That they'd escaped with their lives. Cruelly, that didn't seem to be the case.

Pearla stepped forward, placing a hand on Sev's arm. "What's the treatment?" she asked the doctors. "What can you do for him?"

The man consulted his holopad. "Lumiers," he replied confidently. "This treatment is a standard of Ocarri medicine, and we've had excellent results."

Sev sighed in relief. "When can you start? And when will he be better?"

The doctor folded his hands in front of him. "We can start right away, of course. Lumiers will keep him comfortable. We could heal him in, oh…a year, maybe a little more."

Soren hung his head. There was that phrase again. *Keep him comfortable.* Just like they did with his mother, and she never woke up again.

Sev made a little noise, shocked by the timeframe. "A year? A standard year?"

Soren cleared his throat, gathering his courage in front of the doctors. "There is another option," he said. "Something that would work within a week, maybe less. But there's a problem."

She looked at him hopefully. Another doctor stepped in. "Young Soren speaks out of turn," he said sternly, and gave Soren a stern look. "There is no other way but Lumiers."

"That's not true," Soren said, his eyes hardening. He was tired of being looked over, of being told to be quiet. This family deserved to hear every option, as unlikely as they seemed. "If we had spores from Terra Firma, we could make a serum to counteract the virus. It would go to work almost instantly."

Sev's eyes filled with hope. She looked from Soren to the lead doctor, anxious to hear them out.

"There is no way to Terra Firma," another doctor chimed in. "No one can go there. No one can get the spores. The Council of Planets forbids it."

Sev looked at her father. He looked so broken, so small and weak…not the strong, kind, and loving man she knew. She looked back at the doctors.

"I can go to Terra Firma. I can get the spores."

One doctor laughed. "The Council forbids it, child. And even if you could go, you would likely not survive the return."

Sev narrowed her eyes. She clinched her fists at her sides and stood as tall as she could. "I've been to Terra Firma before. Twice," she spat. "And I could go again."

The room went silent save for the beeps and whirs of the machinery keeping Phoenix alive. Someone gasped.

Soren's eyes went wide. Before he could say anything, another doctor intervened. "You've been exposed to spores on Terra Firma?"

Sev said nothing, defiant as ever. The lead doctor pointed to Soren. "Take her to quarantine," he ordered him.

Soren stepped back, shaking his head. "No," he argued. "She's not sick."

The doctor pushed him out of the way. He called two other medics to come forth, and they pulled Sev away from Pearla.

"No!" Pearla yelled, putting herself between Sev and the medics. "You can't take her. Her father needs her. Please."

A doctor restrained Pearla, and two more medics grabbed Sev. She didn't resist, but tears welled in her eyes as they led her away.

Soren stood frozen, watching. Sev looked back, her gaze locking onto his. Defiant, but just a little afraid.

Something in his chest twisted.

The doctor turned on him with barely restrained disgust. "I'll deal with you later, young man."

Then they were gone.

Soren exhaled sharply, his pulse hammering. They expected him to follow, to do his job. But he couldn't move.

He could still see Pearla, hunched over Phoenix's bed, weeping. He could still see Sev's eyes burning with emotion as they separated her from her family.

His hands curled into fists. The blood rushed in his ears.

Instead of following, he turned and walked back to his office, more conflicted than ever.

CHAPTER 9

Soren sat at his desk, reviewing case notes. The Lumiers for Phoenix would begin tomorrow and thus would start a long and excruciating process of waiting for him to get better, if he got better at all.

What his colleagues didn't like to admit was that Lumiers was a hit-or-miss treatment. When it worked, it worked splendidly, albeit slowly. When it failed, the patient usually died. Granted, this didn't happen often, but it had happened with his mother, and Soren didn't trust it.

He trusted Ocarri medicine less and less, the more patients he treated.

It was near midnight, and he struggled to keep his eyes open. He was well into his double shift by now, but his caseload was light. The doctors had assigned him Phoenix, but there was little to do for him except check the sensors and make sure his nutrition and hydration lines were clear.

At the thought of nutrition, his stomach rumbled. He had not had dinner; just a quick snack here and there. His thoughts turned to Sev. Had she had dinner? Quarantine was an isolating and lonely experience. The thought of her alone, imprisoned and away from her family, made his chest twinge with regret.

He should've done more. He should've challenged the lead doctor. And now things were worse.

He eyed his chair in the corner; just an hour ago he'd tried to sleep. His blanket still lay draped over the back of it.

He tried to concentrate on his notes. He activated his holopad, dictating instructions for Phoenix's Lumiers treatment.

But Soren couldn't concentrate. His fingers wandered to the medical records database almost automatically. He keyed in Sev's name.

Medical Quarantine. Indefinite.

It was the worst possible news. Most medical quarantines lasted forty-eight hours…a few days at most. Sev had no release date.

He turned off the holopad. Soren walked over to the chair, gathered up the blanket, and made his way to the containment suite.

Sev thought of her father. She thought of Pearla.

She was alone in the stark holding cell. There was a thin cot, a sink and toilet, and little else. They had taken her chrono. She had no idea what time it was, but it felt late.

Pearla needed her. Her father needed her. She knew that. Her place was by their side, not caged like an animal.

Unbidden, hot, angry tears filled her eyes, but she swiped them away. She would not cry like this. She would not feel helpless.

For hours, she had beat on the door, demanding they let her out. She'd gotten no reply. It had done nothing but exhausted her. For now, she was too tired to fight.

She wrapped her arms around her body. She was cold; the previous warmth of the Ocarro Medical Center was long gone. She missed Dobani, with its hot sand and sun-drenched afternoons. She missed her bed and their lives before they came to this wretched place.

Sev did her best to rest, but she did not sleep.

The halls were empty. Most night shift workers were attending patients or relaxing in the breakroom between calls. Soren's steps slowed as he got closer and closer to the holding cell. What if she didn't want to see him? What if she was angry?

He shook his head. Of course, she was angry. They had taken her from her family while her father lay gravely ill. She had every right.

He stopped outside her door. It was dark within. He dared not look in the observation window yet. His stomach flipped with anticipation, and he nearly turned around to go back to his office.

He did not. Soren looked through the darkened glass, his hand on the security panel.

She was on her side, facing the wall on that uncomfortable-looking cot. They'd taken her clothes, and she wore an Ocarri medical tunic instead. She looked so cold, the way she curled in on herself. So small. He could see her pale hair in the low light, but beyond that, she was barely visible.

Soren swallowed, his throat thick with emotion.

The blanket felt heavy in his hands. He shifted on his feet. He took his badge, and his hand shook. With a steadying breath, he swiped the security panel. There was a faint beep, and the door clicked open.

The room flooded with harsh light, and Soren stepped inside. Sev rolled over immediately and sat on the edge of the cot. She rubbed her eyes sleepily and looked up at him.

"It's you," she said simply.

Soren didn't know what to say. He stepped forward and held out the blanket. "Thought you could use this."

Sev looked at him guardedly. Soren could see her sit up just a little straighter, almost bracing herself. Her eyes flashed. "Are you here to test me? Draw blood?"

Soren shook his head. "No, Sev. I'm just here. That's all."

She blinked up at him with her large green eyes, gone lighter in the harsh lighting of the cell. "Oh," she replied.

He closed the distance between them. Carefully, Soren draped the blanket around her shoulders, and she shut her eyes. She held the edges and pulled it closer around her. "Thanks," she muttered. She scooted over on the cot, making a place for him. "Make yourself comfortable."

Soren made a face. Sev smiled, a little lopsided. "It was a joke."

He huffed a laugh and took his place beside her. She was not as small as she looked; she was slim but strong. Sev held her shoulders with pride, even as she huddled under his blanket.

"How is my dad?"

Soren looked down before answering. "There's been no change."

Sev nodded, looking a little crestfallen. "Is what you said true? Can you make a serum? Can you save my dad?"

Soren looked serious. "Yes, Sev. I know I could. If we could get spores, that is."

He studied her face. She had deceptively delicate features, but there was strength there. Intelligence. "Were you really on Terra Firma?"

Sev pressed her lips together. "Yeah, I was there. Before the ban, of course." She looked at him then, passion and resolve lighting her eyes. "I can go again," she said, her voice filled with conviction. "I can get them, Soren. But I need your help."

Soren considered. "How would you get there? Travel to Terra Firma is—"

"Forbidden," Sev finished, exasperated. "Yeah, I know. But if I could get back to Dobani, I have a ship. It's mine and my fathers. I know how to fly it."

Soren looked at her, a little awestruck. Sev was so young, but she had a multitude of life experiences behind her. He believed her when she said she could do it. Looking at her there on that cot, with her eyes bright and determined, he believed she could do anything.

He looked away. It would mean defying his colleagues, the rules on Ocarro. He would risk his career and maybe even his life. If they caught him, his life would be over.

Soren looked into her eyes; they were large, warm, and pleading. If he'd had the chance to save his mother, he would've surely taken it, without hesitation.

"Ok," Soren breathed. "Let's do this."

CHAPTER 10

The walk back to his office was eternal. He'd left Sev in her cell very much the way he had found her…curled up on that thin cot. This time she was warm, though, and it eased him some.

And he had a plan. It would work, but they had to act fast. Before dawn, if possible, when the staff was thin, and patients were asleep.

On his way back, he detoured by Phoenix's room. He looked in on him…the woman was still there, ever stalwart at his bedside. She rested her head on her arms over the bed; she might even be asleep. He eased his way in, and she immediately sat up.

Soren greeted her warmly, then crossed to Phoenix. The gentle hum of the machines was the only sound in the room…that droning sound that was both hopeful and despairing. He remembered it from when his mother was sick. The sound of the machines meant she was alive…but at what cost, and to what end?

He looked down at him. Phoenix was pale; he appeared very frail. He checked the sensor readouts for any change. There was none.

"How is he?" the woman asked hopefully. Her voice was wobbly with exhaustion.

Soren looked at her, his eyes soft. "He's stable," he said, trying to make the news sound better than it was. The woman wasn't stupid. Her shoulders dropped at his words.

"What can I do for you?" Soren asked her. "Can I get you something to eat?"

The woman shook her head. "I just want him well," she said. She looked up, eyes roving over his face. "How is Sev? Have you seen her?"

Soren smiled. "Sev is well. She's not sick."

The woman sighed in relief. "When can you release her? I want her to be here when her father wakes up."

Soren narrowed his eyes. He hoped for their sake that Phoenix did wake up, but after the Lumiers tomorrow, he doubted it. He thought of his plan…of Sev's risky escape. "I'm working on that," he replied.

She smiled. "I'm Pearla," the woman said.

He gave her a small smile. "I'm Soren. It's nice to meet you, Pearla."

She inclined her head. Tears had gathered there, but she blinked them away. "How bad is he?" she asked him.

Soren lowered his head. "He's critical. I won't lie to you. And the treatment tomorrow…well I fear it's only going to make matters worse."

Pearla's lower lip quivered before she bit down on it, as if holding back a sob. "I can't lose him," she whispered.

She dropped her gaze, blinking rapidly, willing the tears away. Soren saw the effort, the quiet battle she fought to stay composed, and it made his chest tighten.

Pearla looked up, and Soren locked eyes with her. "You won't," he promised. "But a year out of life is too much of a sacrifice for a chance at a cure. Not when there are other ways."

Pearla nodded, her expression distant. Soren watched her carefully, noting the flicker of recognition in her eyes. She must have remembered what he'd said to the other doctors before they took Sev away.

He could only hope she still believed in him—that he could help them both.

Soren was halfway to the door. "I can't say more about it…not yet. I'll return when I can. Stay strong, Pearla."

He left her standing there, her gaze lingering on him. Soren didn't look back, but he could sense her uncertainty, the way she seemed to be searching for meaning in his words.

◆ ◆ ◆

Sev dozed. She knew she would need rest if she was ever getting off this planet. She didn't know what Soren had planned, but she trusted him.

It was unusual for her to be so trusting, but something about him seemed sincere. She believed he genuinely wanted to help. It felt right.

But it had been hours since he'd promised to return. *Where had he gone?* She wondered. She worried he had forgotten her.

Sev burrowed further into the blanket. It was supple and smelled like Soren. The scent was comforting and strangely familiar; it reminded her of when she would fall asleep on the couch at home and would wake up under her father's blanket. It soothed an anxious part of her, allowing her to close her eyes and rest.

Sometime later, Sev heard footsteps in the hall outside her cell. She tensed; her eyes went wide in the dark, and her breath quickened.

A shadow passed under the door, and she gasped. Whoever it was, they were coming inside.

More tests, she thought miserably. She scooted back on the cot, trying to appear as small as possible.

The security panel beeped, and the door swung open. A dark shadow stood stark against the light in the hall. Sev's heart beat faster, and she wrapped the blanket tightly around her.

The overhead lights blinked on, and Soren stepped forth. He was holding her clothes and chrono, along with a coat and boots.

Sev sighed in relief. She stood, meeting him halfway. "I thought you'd forgotten me," she whispered a little breathlessly.

Soren's mouth twitched in a half smile, his black eyes reflecting the light. "Not likely, Sev."

She blinked at him. His gaze made her feel strangely seen…made her stomach flip in a way she was entirely unfamiliar with. It was not unpleasant.

"Here," Soren said, breaking the moment. "I brought you these. You're going to need them where you're going."

He held out her clothes, the coat and boots. "Let's get you dressed, hmm? We've got to hurry."

Sev nodded. He turned his back, and she slipped into her clothes. She shrugged on the coat. It was twice her size, but it was warm. The boots too were a little big, but she tested them and found that she could walk fine.

"Thank you," she breathed, and he turned back around. She pulled the coat tightly around her, the tie hanging loose. Soren took the ends of it and secured them around her middle.

Sev flushed. She placed her hand atop his, stilling his movements. He looked up at her, their faces close.

"What will happen to you" Sev asked him. Her green eyes flashed in question; his hands were warm beneath hers.

Soren smiled. "Nothing," he said, "unless we get caught."

Sev nodded. Soren tugged her by the hand. "Let's go," he whispered, and they snuck into the hall together.

The hall was bright…too bright. Soren led them down the twisting pathways by supply closets and patient rooms. He headed toward the exit, and Sev stopped him.

"My dad," she whispered. "I can't leave without seeing him." She looked up at him, jade eyes shining. "Please, Soren."

He swallowed, then nodded. Sev watched him closely, sensing something shift behind his eyes, something unspoken, but heavy.

Was he thinking of someone? The thought struck her suddenly, and her chest tightened. Maybe that was why he was helping her now. Maybe he understood what it meant to lose someone too soon, to not get the chance to say goodbye.

He turned them down the hall that would lead them to Phoenix's room. Sev spied Pearla through the door. She was sitting rigidly in that uncomfortable chair beside Phoenix's bed. She had her arms crossed in front of her.

Soren opened the door. Pearla looked up, surprised to see him again so soon. Then Sev stepped out from behind him.

"Oh, Drek be praised!" she exclaimed. Sev rushed to her, wrapping her in a warm hug. "Pearla," she breathed. "I'm going to Terra Firma…I'm going to get the spores."

Pearla withdrew. She searched her face, her eyes filled with tears. "Sev, how? How can you go when it's forbidden?"

Sev smiled. "The skiff. If I can get back home, I can take the skiff."

Pearla gasped. "By yourself? Oh Sev, I can't lose you too!"

Sev pulled away, holding her by the shoulders. "You haven't lost anybody yet, Pearla."

Pearla looked at Soren. "You'll make sure she has safe passage to Dobani?"

Soren nodded solemnly. "You have my word." He looked at Sev, his eyes soft. "I believe in her," he said with a smile. "I know she can do this, or I wouldn't have helped."

Sev looked back at Soren, appreciation lighting her eyes. She leaned in and kissed Pearla's cheek. "Stay strong for Daddy," she whispered. "And remember me in your prayers."

Pearla nodded. She felt a tear escape her lashes, and she wiped it away.

Sev moved to her father's bed. She leaned over him, holding her father's hand. "Daddy? Daddy, I need you to hear me."

She watched Phoenix for any sign of life. His fingers twitched at the sound of her voice, but he made no move to wake.

"I'm kind of glad you're asleep, Daddy. You'd try to talk me out of this otherwise."

She looked at her father's sleeping face, his furrowed brow. The air hose hummed beside them, the beep of the sensors keeping time with his breaths.

Sev leaned close to his ear. "I love you so, so much, Phoenix. More than I ever dreamed I could love anyone." Sev felt tears sting her eyes. She let them flow freely. "I'm leaving. But I'll be back…and you'll be better."

She felt a hand rest gently on her shoulder. "Sev," Soren said urgently. "We have to go. We don't have much time."

She nodded quickly, wiping the tears away. She leaned forward and gave her father a gentle kiss on his cheek. His skin was dry and feverish. "Hold on for me," she whispered before pulling away.

A silver thread made its way down the side of his face. Sev turned from him and followed Soren out of the room. She did not look back.

♦ ♦ ♦

Soren led her through the winding halls and outside onto the Medical Center property. The snow crunched beneath her feet, and the biting wind chapped her face. Soren walked her through the blizzard, past the transport pad, beyond the frozen lake, up to the edge of the valley.

He held her shoulders, directing her to look at him. "I can't go with you any further," he said regrettably. The wind howled around them. Soren suddenly didn't want her to leave…he felt the anxious pull of her loss deep in his chest.

He reached and adjusted her collar, pulling the too-big coat closer around her. Sev looked at him from the fur-lined hood, her eyes bright, a tender smile on her face. Over the mountains, the sun was rising pink and orange and buttercream, spilling light down into the valley.

"Take care of my father," she told him.

Soren nodded. "Take care of yourself."

Sev grinned. She hitched up her pack, turning to go. Soren caught her arm.

He'd told himself this was about Phoenix. About wanting to save a grieving family from the same fate he'd endured. But watching her walk away, he realized it was more than that.

"There's a shipping barge over the mountain. My uncle owns it. It's headed for Dobani tomorrow. Make sure you're on it."

Sev nodded. She had pushed back the hood, and the morning sun was streaming through her blonde hair, setting it on fire. "Thank you," she mouthed to him, and he let her go. He stood there watching as she faded into the valley, swallowed by light.

CHAPTER 11

He took the long way back, where he would hopefully go undetected by the Medical Center security. Not that he wasn't free to do as he pleased, but if external cameras caught him outside of the center, they might suspect him of taking part in Sev's disappearance.

As for being caught at all, he honestly had not thought that far ahead.

The back entrance of the Medical Center loomed in front of him. On either side of the door, he could see two white-clad medical personnel. *Probably doctors on a stim break*, he thought.

As he got closer to the entrance, the doctors assembled. Only they weren't doctors at all. They were Ocarri security bots in white uniforms, and they were walking toward him.

Panic straightened his spine. He thought of running, but he knew he wouldn't get far. He turned around, trying to look casual, only to walk right into the energy field of a security drone.

The field crackled around him, holding him in place. Snow billowed outside his transparent prison. He thought of Sev, who was an off-worlder and unused to the brutal conditions here. He silently hoped she was ok…that she would make it despite the odds.

Soren slowly turned around to face his fate. Four security bots stood between him and the door, trapping him.

Just then, several doctors walked out onto the snowy plain, headed straight for him. One of them was Carlin, the lead doctor, followed by Prescott, his kind old mentor. Carlin held a blanket.

But it wasn't just a blanket. It was his blanket…the one he'd given Sev.

Oh, he thought bleakly. *It's truly over now.*

Carlin looked at him smugly and held the blanket just out of his reach. "Recognize this?"

Soren said nothing. He looked at Carlin defiantly, his eyes hard.

"I recognize it," Carlin continued. "It's the blanket from your office. I've seen it many times. Isn't that right, Prescott?"

Prescott nodded, albeit a little hesitantly. "It's his blanket, yes," he conceded. "But I feel he gave it to the girl in what began as an act of kindness."

Carlin scowled, then looked toward the security bots. "Bring him to my office," he ordered them.

The bots led Soren through the back entrance and down the hall to Carlin's office. Prescott was close behind, and he felt reassured by his old mentor's presence.

Carlin dismissed them and gestured for Soren to sit in a chair opposite his desk. Prescott, ever staunch and supportive, sat in the other one.

"How could you do this, Soren? You know the rules. You swore to abide by them. Now, you've put us all at risk."

Soren could be silent no longer. He shook his head. "Sev isn't sick. She never was. She should get to come and go as she pleases."

Carlin pointed at Soren, aggressively stabbing the air. "That was not your call to make, young man. The medical council's methodology is clear. If she is truly not infectious, we would've found out in due time."

Soren huffed. "By when? By the time her father dies?"

"Now Soren—" Prescott began, but Soren waved him off.

"I only wanted to help Sev. Like I wanted to help her father. But you wouldn't let me help either of them. Ocarri medicine used to be about healing the sick…helping the weary."

He stopped speaking, his eyes alight with passion. He stood, approaching Carlin's desk and placing his hands on the edge. "And that's what I swore an oath to do," he said. "To help people. Not to serve your senseless rules. If what I did was wrong, I'm not worried about being right."

Prescott had a small smile on his face. Carlin looked on, disappointed.

"Might I say something?"

Both Carlin and Soren looked at the older man. His speaking up surprised Soren, but it didn't displease him.

"Soren is one of our brightest young medics," Prescott began. "He has performed admirably over the course of his tenure here. He has saved many lives."

"With Ocarri medicine, though," Carlin added, as if trying to prove a point.

Prescott demurred. "With Ocarri medicine, yes. But I suspect he could've done it without Ocarri help."

Carlin frowned. "What are you trying to say, Prescott? That Soren broke protocol because he's *talented?* Because I think it's because he's a dissenter. And dissenters don't do well here, and they surely don't have a place in medicine."

Soren swallowed. Dissenters on Ocarri went to prison. They worked their fingers to the bone in mining colonies and prison work camps. His father had died in one such camp. Working to build a life apart from the shame of that family label had taken Soren most of his childhood and all his adult life. But he wouldn't betray his father's memory by denying it.

The old doctor looked at Soren, his lips turned down. "I'm sorry, Soren. I did what I could."

Carlin activated the comm. The security bots returned, coming to stand behind Soren. "Take the dissenter away," Carlin ordered.

The bots grabbed Soren. He did not resist. He knew what could happen when he helped Sev, and he didn't regret it. More than that, he was proud of it. And if it saved Phoenix, then that's even better.

They led him out of the office, but he turned around at the threshold. "Promise me you'll help him, Prescott. Promise me."

Soren saw his hesitation. It was no small thing that Soren asked of him…he knew that. It was a risk to be associated with the ideology of a dissenter. But after a few breaths, Prescott nodded. It soothed him.

The bots pointed him down the hall. They passed his old office and Phoenix's treatment room. Pearla saw them pass and stood, alarmed. She locked eyes with him, no doubt wondering what had happened.

Soren smiled. He'd done what he'd set out to do, and that was enough.

◆ ◆ ◆

Sev had known cold growing up in the icy expanse of the Black. She knew the discomfort of the Dobani off season. Sev had never known cold like this.

The wind howled, and the snow swirled around her in thick drifts. Day wore on into evening. The blinding white of the landscape she traversed became muted with the mellow colors of approaching night. The sunset reminded her of her beloved beach back home, but the comparisons stopped there.

A blast of cutting wind sliced across her face, nearly taking her breath. While Soren's jacket was warm and the hood protective, there was nothing shielding her nose and cheeks from the biting wind. They burned with cold, tingling and numb at the same time.

Her stomach growled. Sev was no stranger to hunger, but she knew if she did not eat soon, her body would grow weak. She would need to be strong if she was to make it to Dobani.

The slope of the trail increased dramatically, and she struggled to keep her footing. She had to get to the top before nightfall. Winds on the southern side were brutal, and with no shelter, she knew she wouldn't make the night.

She had seen no living creatures on her trek…no vegetation. She wondered briefly how the Ocarri sustained themselves if there were no animals to hunt or berries to gather. Did they grow their food indoors, like they did their medicine? Perhaps.

A powerful gust of wind nearly blew her backwards, and she hugged the surface of the mountain, trying not to fall. She reached up to grab a jagged rock for leverage; she noticed her fingers had gone white with cold. Sev only knew they'd landed on the rock when she could see them on its surface. All sensation was gone.

With significant effort, she pulled herself up. The sun was setting over the top of the mountain. She had twenty, maybe thirty more feet until the summit.

Then Sev stepped wrong, and her ankle twisted. She slid a few terrifying feet down the slope, but her fingers caught the edge of a rock, halting her momentum. She cried out, fearful of falling and in pain from her injured ankle.

Sev felt the tears stinging her eyes before she realized it. What if this injury was the beginning of the end? What if, in her foolish youthful bravado, she'd doomed her father to die? They'd find her body frozen to this mountain, and she'd never seen Phoenix again.

The tears never fell. She resolved not to cry. *No,* she thought with determination, *not like that.*

With grit and determination, she scrambled her way up the rest of the distance, tearing through the snow and dragging her ankle like a dead weight.

Sev reached the top just as the sun slipped below the horizon, plunging the sky into a blue-black darkness.

It was flat at the top, desolate and snowy. Stars blinked onto the blank canvas of the night sky, clear and luminous. To her left, a large outcropping of rocks jutted out from the mountain…it wasn't much, but it would do to weather the night.

Sev limped over to the outcropping and ducked under it. The ground was dry and free of snow, and she was grateful. She drew her legs up close to her body and lay on her side against the hard earth. Her ankle throbbed…she could feel it swelling in her boot. She reached beyond the outcropping and took a handful of snow. With a wince, she stuffed it into her sock, hoping it would relieve some of the swelling.

Exhaustion overtook her. She placed her hands in the pockets of her coat, and though her fingers were mostly numb, she felt something there. She concentrated on closing her fingers around it and pulling it out.

It was a ration bar. Soren must've put it there before he gave her his jacket. Sev smiled.

She fumbled with the wrapper, her numb fingers making even the most mundane tasks difficult. When she could finally take a bite, she couldn't stop the little noise of contentment that escaped her.

When she finished the ration bar, she curled into the coat and tried to rest. Her back was to the wind, and though she had no fire, she would not freeze. It wouldn't be the most comfortable night she's spent, but she was determined not to die in this barren land.

Then, a noise mixed in among the howling wind. It was a high-pitched and mournful sound; something lean and hungry lurked among the rocks.

She shivered and burrowed deeper into her coat. Sev sent up a silent prayer to Drek or anyone listening that she wouldn't be a meal for the night creatures here.

Squinting in the dark, she scanned the horizon for any sign of them. From the space below the outcropping, Sev could see the stars. It reminded her of the times she and her father had slept out in the open and, in that patient way of his, he had told her of the constellations and what they meant to the cultures on various planets.

She refused to believe they wouldn't share such experiences again, or that her father wouldn't return to his full health. After all, that's why she was doing this.

She tried to rest. The night had grown darker; she could barely make out the snow amid the shadows. When she finally succumbed to sleep, it was to chase warmer dreams and with a wistful desire for her bed back on Dobani.

CHAPTER 12

Phoenix was underfoot, as usual, clinging to the hem of his mother's dress. The dust from the flour on the floor billowed around him, dusting his hands and settling in his hair.

His mother stood at the kitchen counter, working the dough with her hands. Phoenix had pulled the flour sack out of the cupboard and had made quite a mess.

He patted his hands on the little mound of flour and let out a peal of giggles. It got his mother's attention, and she looked down at him.

"Oh! I can't leave you for a second, you rascal!" She picked him up, transferring the white dust from his overalls to the front of her apron. She kissed his cheek, thumbing away a smudge of flour. "Did Drek's kiss spread over your whole body, Feenie? Hmm? Is that what happened?"

Phoenix placed his hand against his mother's face and smiled. His grin was the lopsided and carefree grin of a toddler, dotted with sparse teeth.

His mother placed him on the floor and pulled up a chair. Phoenix struggled to climb onto it, finally raising his hands to her for help. She picked him up and stood him next to her. "There you are, Feenie. You want to play in flour so much, you can help me make biscuits, eh?"

Phoenix pressed his hands into the dough he could now reach, squealing with delight. Through the window, the morning sun was streaming into the warm kitchen, blanketing everything in ribbons of light. Phoenix looked at his mother. She'd tied up her dark hair, but tendrils fell around her face, catching the sun. Her lips were red and glossy. Phoenix clasped a handful of dough and showed it to her, proud of his efforts. She took the bit of dough and rolled into a ball before placing it into a greased and floured pan. "That one can be yours, little one," she told him softly.

Phoenix continued to play, content, and his mother sang low and sweet until she had rolled out all the biscuits and put them in the oven.

Somewhere, from far away, there was a distant whir of machinery…the drip-drop of water. Phoenix looked around and he was no longer in the kitchen of his childhood home. He was in the yard, kicking up dirt.

"You always win, Phoenix! Can't you let me win just one time?"

Lorien canted his head, his dark eyes and dark hair a perfect match for his brother.

Phoenix grinned. "It's not fair play to let someone win, Lori. Don't you want the satisfaction of a well-played game?"

Lorien frowned. "But I'm little. Mama said you are too quick to forget that." He put his hands on his hips as if to prove his point.

Phoenix smiled a little crookedly. He wore a newsboy cap, but Drek's kiss still stuck out from under it. "Fair enough, fair enough. Let's start again, and I'll give you a full minute's advance. Good deal?"

Lorien's dark eyes brightened, and a sizeable smile spread across his cherubic face. He nodded, his excitement palpable.

They lined up their rocks at the starting line. Phoenix gave Lorien the stick, and he let him go first. Lorien pushed his rock along in the dirt, happily looking back to see if Phoenix was chasing him yet.

On the porch, their father was reading the Sunday paper. He looked out over it, his glasses pushed down on his nose. "Phoenix!" he called roughly, and Phoenix snapped his head in his direction. "C'mere."

Phoenix shoved his hands in his pockets. Behind him, Lorien was still pushing his rock across the dusty yard. A knot of dread formed in his stomach as he approached his father. He was a tall, imposing man who detested what he called "foolishness." Once, when Phoenix had spilled his cider, he'd said nothing. The next day, he made him join him in the fields at dawn, a whole hour earlier than they usually worked.

He arrived before his father and shifted a little on his feet. His father's pipe sat on a table by his chair, a little blue curl of smoke coiling from it. Phoenix focused on that, rather than his father's face, when he finally spoke.

"Sir?"

His father leaned forward, uncrossing his legs. "You make sure you let Lorien win, you hear me, boy?"

Phoenix bit his lip. He nodded furiously. His father looked at him expectantly.

"Now, what do you say to me, Phoenix? I want to hear it."

Phoenix exhaled a breath he didn't know he was holding, but his chest still felt tight. "Yes sir," he said, quiet but sure.

His father leaned back in his rocking chair, unfolding his paper once again, and continued reading.

When he turned back toward the yard, Lorien had stopped the race. He was looking curiously at Phoenix.

Phoenix returned to the starting point, and Lorien walked back to meet him. Lorien leaned in. "Are you in trouble, Feenie?" His eyes were wide and questioning.

Phoenix pulled his brother into a quick hug. "No Lori," he mumbled. "Everything is fine." He released him, then picked up his own stick. "Let's go again," Phoenix told him with a smile. "Fair is fair."

Phoenix tried to speak…tried to move. He hadn't seen his brother Lorien in decades. His sweet brother Lorien. The scene grew dark. When he opened his eyes again, he was running through the fields with Lorien. They were older. They had their arms out, pretending to be spaceships. Lorien was making noises with his mouth, simulating the sounds of taking off and landing.

Phoenix was laughing. They were both barefoot. Lorien caught up to him; he was much older now. His dark hair had grown lighter, while Phoenix's remained unchanged. Lorien tackled him in the rows of wheat, knocking him to the ground.

They both giggled until they were out of breath. Phoenix sat up, and Lorien followed. Phoenix had a sandwich in his pocket. He pulled it out and discovered that it hadn't gotten smashed in their tussling.

Lorien smiled. "Let's share it anyway," he said, and Phoenix agreed. He gave half to Lorien and kept the more damaged half for himself.

Lorien sat cross-legged in between the rows opposite Phoenix. They ate as crows cawed overhead, begging for scraps. Lori wiped his mouth on his shirtsleeve and tossed his crust to the birds. The sun was high in the sky; it was the hot months on Venya and the dry season to boot.

"Hey Feenie, let's go swimming!"

Phoenix considered. The river was just down the hill from his father's field. They could swim for a little while and dry off in time for supper.

Phoenix stood and dusted himself off. He held out his hand to his little brother, and Lorien took it and pulled himself up. Together, they ran down the hill toward the river.

Halfway through the glade that hugged the riverbank, Lorien bolted ahead. He was in the water before Phoenix had ever reached the bank.

"Hey Lori! Wait for me!" Phoenix called after him.

Lorien looked back, halfway across the river. "Head start, remember?" he yelled with a big smile. "I'll race you to the other side!"

Anxiety closed around Phoenix's heart to see his little brother so far out in the river alone. Phoenix dove in after him and swam furiously to catch up. The current strengthened, and Phoenix's arms grew tired. All that kept him going was the pale blur of Lorien ahead of him, advancing at a rapid speed.

"Lorien!" Phoenix yelled, "Slow down!" But Lorien did not answer. After a while, Phoenix's legs cramped, but still he swam, trying to catch up to Lorien so he didn't have to cross the river alone.

There was a sharp cry, followed by a splash. Phoenix looked up and saw a small hand disappearing beneath the water.

"No!" Phoenix screamed. He swam faster, fighting the fast-moving water. He dove, frantically searching. The waters on Venya were clear enough for him to see underwater, but there was silt and debris in the river that made searching difficult.

Ahead, beneath a felled log, he saw him.

Phoenix swam, dread souring his stomach. He pulled Lorien's arm from under the log; he must've slipped under and become trapped there.

Phoenix got Lorien under the arms and began dragging him back to the shore. "Come on, Lori…stay with me," he pleaded over and over. "Stay with me! Just a little further, now."

Phoenix reached the bank, so exhausted he could barely pull himself out of the water, let alone Lorien, too. He placed Lorien on the sandy shore. His lips were blue.

Phoenix could barely see for the tears that flooded his eyes. He rolled Lorien over onto his side, and water came pouring out of his mouth. He patted his back…pressed on his stomach, trying anything to wake him up. Lorien did not move except under Phoenix's ministrations.

"Oh Lori," Phoenix cried. "Lori, Lori, please."

Then a little voice inside told him to *run*.

He pressed on Lorien's stomach one more time. His head jostled. His eyes were closed, and his lips were still blue.

Phoenix got up and scrambled up the bank. Getting help was his only thought. If he could get home, he could save Lori. His father would know what to do. His mother. They would know.

Phoenix ran full tilt over rocks and through briars toward home. The sun was deceptively warm and inviting, and the sky was a brilliant blue. When he made it back to the field, he could see his house…he could see his father on the front porch, smoking a pipe.

"Da—," Phoenix tried to say, out of breath and chest aching from running. He looked down, and his feet were bleeding. "Daddy, come quick," he finally managed. "It's Lorien."

His father bolted off the porch. He snatched Phoenix by the shoulders and shook him. "Where is he? What's happened?"

His mother came out onto the porch, wiping her hands on her apron. She looked down at Phoenix's bloodied feet. "Feenie, what have you gotten into, love?"

Although he had never cried in front of his father, he couldn't stop the tears from flowing now. "He's at the river," he managed, and his father's hands on his arms grew tighter. "We w-were swimming."

His father released him and ran toward the field. Phoenix started in after him, hysterical, but his mother seized him and dragged him back into the house.

He was sitting by the fire with a fresh change of clothes and bandaged feet when his father returned to the house. He heard him before he saw him. It was a groaning sound, long and low…an animal sound. Phoenix had never heard his father make that sound or anything near it.

He ran out onto the porch and dropped the blanket his mother had given him. His father walked across the yard with Lorien in his arms. He was limp, his pale limbs hung freely. His head lolled.

His mother gripped the balustrade for balance, one hand over her heart. "Drek's face has turned from us!" she cried. She stumbled forth, trying to reach Lorien. "My baby, my baby," she crooned. "My little baby!"

Phoenix looked on, helpless to do anything but exist in the moment. His mother touched her hand to Lorien's lifeless face and collapsed, overridden with grief.

His father's face was ashen. He gripped his son in his arms like he could imbue him with life by sheer will alone. He looked at Phoenix, his lip trembling. His voice dropped to a hollow whisper. "What have you done?"

Phoenix blinked at him, slowly backing into the house. Tears were streaming down his face. His brother…his little shadow. Gone. *And it was his fault.*

His father's face contorted, and his mouth twisted into a snarl. "Boy, I'm talking to you—what have you *done*?"

◆ ◆ ◆

Phoenix stirred in his sleep. The somber veil of his dream lingered. He opened his eyes to the stark ceiling, then inspected the machines that ticked and hummed around him. He looked down at his body. There was an array of sensors, tubes, and hoses. *"Race you to the other side!"* he heard Lorien say, and he tried to blink it away.

The door opened, and it was Pearla. His Pearla. She looked so tired. She was holding a cup of stim.

When she saw him, she rushed to his bedside. "Phoenix? You're awake! Stars alive!"

She reached for his hand, and he clutched it as best he could. He blinked away the cobwebs of his dreams…memories he had kept long buried. Moments from his past that had remained dormant most of his adult life.

"S-Sev," he managed, and Pearla retrieved a cup of water and raised it to his lips. He took a grateful sip. "Where is she?"

Pearla looked through the windows to see if anyone in the hall was listening. They were alone. She leaned close to his ear. "She's gone to Terra Firma to find spores for your cure."

Tears filled his eyes. "No," he whispered. "Not Sev too. Not little mouse, too," he cried.

Pearla shushed him. "It's ok, love. She's doing it for you. So you can be better. So we can be home again."

Phoenix shook his head. "Gone," he said miserably. "Lorien's gone."

Pearla climbed into the bed, curling up alongside him. He continued to cry. "Sev's gone. Lorien's gone," he whispered.

Pearla wiped a tear from her eye. She didn't know all the secret hurts that haunted Phoenix, but she wouldn't let him face them alone.

She lay against the pillow beside him until he fell back to sleep, the beeps of the machines lulling them both into an uneasy sort of peace.

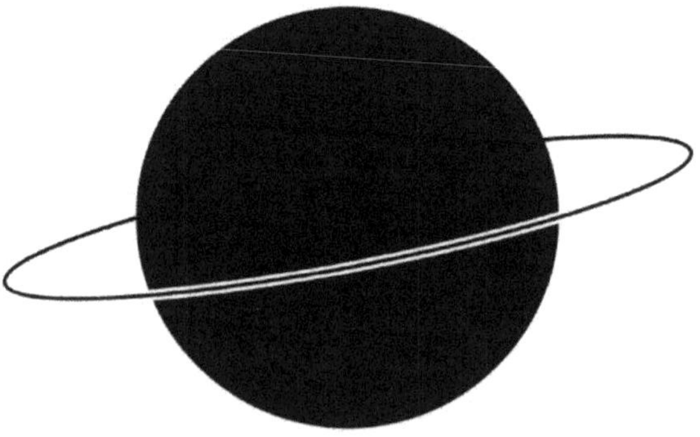

CHAPTER 13

S ev awoke to a blinding sunrise. The morning sun spilled over the top of the mountain range, painting the blank canvas of the snowy planet in pink and yellow hues. It was as beautiful as any Dobani sunrise she'd ever seen, or slightly more than. She took a moment to appreciate a moment of peace in this stark and dangerous place.

She stretched in her little alcove and tested her ankle. The swelling was much improved; the snow had done its job.

Sev crawled out from under the outcropping. There would be no magically appearing ration bars this morning, she thought with regret. She scooped up some snow, let it melt in her hand and sipped the resulting water. That would have to do.

She pulled Soren's coat tightly around her and tightened the laces of her boots. She looked over the edge of the mountain, down into the surrounding valley. There was less snow on this side. It was rocky and promised to be a precarious descent. With a steadying breath, she started her way down, picking her way through the brush and stubby grasses. Her ankle still twinged, but it would hold her weight. She pushed through the pain, making her way down the mountain.

Down below, she saw a small, furry creature foraging in the brush. It made her smile. This was the first time (besides hearing the terrifying night creatures) that she'd seen evidence of animal life on Ocarro. It gave her hope that this ball of ice had a softer side…a more familiar and habitable side. Until now, Ocarro had been quite unforgiving.

The little creature spied her and skipped away to disappear into its burrow. It was warmer on this side of the mountain…still frigid, but the sun was welcome on her back, and her fingers were no longer numb.

After a few more hours of tedious descent, Sev saw the barge where it sat hovering in the valley. The repulsor jets were engaged, signifying it was close to take off. A flash of alarm threatened to overtake her. What if she didn't make it in time? What if the transport took off without her? And what if this wasn't the transport going to Dobani, and she ended up stranded and alone on an alien planet just when her father needed her most?

She blinked it away. Now was not the time to panic. She had to stay focused. Sev hurried, gritting her teeth against the pain in her ankle. When she finally reached the bottom of the mountain, she crouched behind a thick stand of bushes and watched.

Workers were moving in and out of the shipping container, loading and unloading supplies. She'd have to be stealthy if she was going to sneak onboard. If she allowed herself to be caught, then Phoenix would surely die.

A whistle blew, signifying the luncheon hour. Sev watched as the workers congregated near the front of the ship, clearing the shipping container hatch.

She broke cover and ran for it, trying not to scream at the pain in her ankle. She was limping by the time she reached the barge. Her heart started beating double-time. The compartment was more than waist-high, and she could barely reach it. She had to be quick or get caught.

Sev jumped as best as she could on one foot, grabbing the lip of the container hatch with the tips of her fingers. The cold steel bit into her fingertips. She could feel herself slipping. *No no no,* she chanted internally. Her boots dangled over the valley, scraping the sides of the barge. Then suddenly, a shout echoed from the other side…a worker returning early from lunch. Their footsteps crunched across the frozen grass, and Sev held her breath, willing herself to hang on. Her fingers ached. Her mind flashed to being thirteen. She'd fallen off her scooter. "Pain is just noise, little mouse," Phoenix had said as he bandaged her knee. "Drown out the noise."

With one last burst of strength, she pulled herself up and climbed into the dark compartment. It was dusty and filled with large crates of goods. Sev found a place near the back of the compartment and wedged herself between one crate and the wall of the barge. Best to make herself small, she thought. *Be small, stay undetectable.*

She shivered. It was chillier on the barge. The unyielding steel floor of the ship held a biting sort of cold. She pulled her knees up to her chest and rested her head there. After a few moments, the whistle blew again, and the workers returned to their tasks. Sev listened and watched, but no one came near her hiding place. For the first time in a long time, she could relax.

◆ ◆ ◆

Soren lay on the thin cot, staring at the water-stained ceiling. A single bulb there flickered, strobe-like and intermittent, chasing the shadows of his cell.

He had his fingers laced over his middle. He was exhausted, but he could not sleep. The wet cold of the cell had seeped into his bones…it was all he could do to keep from shaking. He instinctively curled his fingers, but they were stiff with cold, and he instantly thought better of it.

Though his body craved rest, his mind was wide awake. All he could think of was Sev, of her climbing a mountain in a borrowed coat. She was an off-worlder accustomed to warmer temperatures. Soren had sent her off alone in a blizzard. He could only hope she had made it and was on her way to Dobani by now.

His patient, Phoenix, was in far greater danger, he feared. The Ocarri people wanted to help. They wanted to heal. But they wanted to do it their way. That's what worried him most.

The old man across from him had a rattle in his chest. He had not spoken, had not moved from where he faced the wall curled up on his cot.

As if he had summoned him, the old man turned over on his back. "The new ones never have much to say to begin with."

Soren did not reply. He remained there, counting the cracks in the ceiling until the old man spoke again.

"What did they get you for?"

He paused, a coughing fit interrupting him. "I'm guessing you're a dissenter." He turned and looked at Soren. The old man had a cataract over one eye, and its pale blue pall glowed in the low light. "I'm rarely ever wrong."

Soren frowned, hesitating. He didn't trust the man, but he didn't see the harm in answering him, being that they found themselves in the same situation. Soren let the silence grow weighty between them until it became unbearable.

He cleared his throat. "I helped someone escape."

The old man huffed, his chest rattling. "Who was she?" he asked him.

Soren turned to face him. "How did you—"

The prisoner waved him off. "It's always a woman," he said gruffly. He pointed at himself. "My name's Cyrus."

Soren gave him his name, and the old man seemed satisfied. Soren was anything but. He wondered about Cyrus and what he'd done to be imprisoned like this. He worried his bottom lip with his teeth, considering if he should pry.

"What did you do, Cyrus? How long have you been here?"

Cyrus gestured with his hands. "Oh, I'm a dissenter, same as you, young man. Reported the curriculum of the government school. I was a teacher there. Told my neighbor it wasn't healthy for my son." The old man sighed, weary and out of breath. In the low light, silver tears shined in his eyes. "They came to get me the next day."

Soren blew out a breath. "You've been here ever since?"

Cyrus nodded. "Every living day for twenty years. These four walls. People come and go. Ocarri, mostly. Sometimes not. But I remain."

"What happens to them?" Soren asked, although he wasn't sure he really wanted to know.

The old man whistled low. "Who knows," he said. He flourished his hand. "Ocarri government wants you gone…poof…you're gone."

Soren swallowed. He did not have any family left. His mother died when he was a child, succumbing to illness at the hands of Ocarri doctors. His father, in an Ocarri prison camp, or so he was told. He never got to say goodbye. The government took him away, and by that time, Soren was training to become a doctor many miles from home. Word of his death came by holopad, remote and impersonal.

Down the hall, there was the staccato sound of footfalls…boots on the stone floor. Guards were making their hourly inspection. Cyrus and Soren fell instinctively quiet, careful not to draw attention to themselves.

After the guards had passed, Soren addressed Cyrus in a more hushed and conservative tone.

"You have a son?"

Cyrus did not answer at first. He grew quiet, reflective. "I had a son," he said. "There was an accident at the school. My son never recovered."

Soren did not press the issue. He closed his eyes, and a reflective sort of peace existed between them. Soren thought of how his career was over…the only thing he really had left. He would never heal the sick again. He would waste away in here until he was old and feeble, like Cyrus.

His lip trembled, but he refused to feel sorry for himself. He clenched his fists until his fingernails dug into his palms, the pain grounding him against hopelessness. Self-pity was the least productive thing he could do, and he wouldn't indulge in it.

"I'm sorry to hear about your son," Soren told him, but it sounded hollow. "I…don't have any children. Or anyone, for that matter."

Cyrus grunted. "Good. Makes doing the time easier when no one is on the outside needing you."

Soren hummed. "My patients need me," he replied. "I can't stay here."

Cyrus appraised him with narrowed eyes, his expression unreadable. He finally huffed a bitter laugh. "Son, you'll stay as long as they say you will." He looked him up and down. Soren now wore the dingy white jumpsuit of dissenters on Ocarri. Cyrus studied him for a moment before curling his lips into a snarl. "Don't look like a doctor to me," he said.

Soren lifted his chin. "I'm a medic. First year. It's what I was born to do. I devoted my life to practicing Ocarri medicine."

"And look where it's gotten you," the old man finished for him. He spat on the concrete floor of their cell, a disgusted look on his face. "That's for Ocarri medicine. For what it's done for me and for what it did for my son."

The old man fell into a coughing fit, and Soren let him be. He could've helped him, had they met under different circumstances. Now, it was no use. Soren couldn't help anyone now. He couldn't even help himself.

CHAPTER 14

His mother had him up early that morning. Villagers had brought food, but it sat in the icebox, undisturbed. His mother did not eat. She barely drank. She ghosted the rooms on quiet feet, absently touching the doorframe, Lorien's seat at the kitchen table. The light in her eyes was gone.

His father sat in his chair by the door. He took his meals in silence, barely touching his food. His mother spoke to him, but he replied in clipped words and aborted sentences. There was a hardness in his eyes. He did not acknowledge Phoenix at all.

The house was quiet without Lorien; there was no ringing laughter, no playful crashes followed by muttered apologies. The house was still. A dark sadness prevailed. There was no joy anymore.

Phoenix, as young as he was, felt it acutely. He felt the absence…the way the house had changed, how the very air had shifted.

The villages only congregated for two events…weddings and funerals. And today, it was the latter.

"Lift your arms, love. There will be a lot of people there today. They will expect you to look a certain way."

Her voice was hollow, not like his mother at all. He raised his arms, and she draped the tunic over him. It was pure white and seamless. His mother wore a white dress that dusted her ankles, and a long white veil.

"Come," she said. "Let's get your father."

They walked together toward the living room where his father sat. He wore a black suit. He was looking off into the distance, but there was nothing there.

"You're not wearing the robes?" his mother asked.

He stood. His father had always been an imposing man, but in that dark suit, he was even more so. "No, I am not, Cordera. I do not find hope in the death of my son."

She bowed her head. Cordera said nothing for a long moment, but the grip on Phoenix's hand tightened. Phoenix looked at her face through the veil. Tears shone on her cheeks.

"Nor do I, Darius. But I will have my son buried in the old ways." She held her head up, resolve evident beneath the grief. "It's what he deserves."

Darius advanced a step or two. "He deserved to live," he said gruffly, and stalked past them to the waiting transport outside.

Phoenix and his mother followed behind, neither of them speaking.

They walked into the gathering hall. Phoenix looked around, his eyes wide. Long drapes covered the windows. The air was smoky…the stone hall was cold and damp. Vaulted ceilings held the village banners, a colorful contrast to the somber proceedings. Villagers from both sides of the aisle canted their head to them…smiled at them. It made Phoenix extremely uncomfortable.

Phoenix's father led them to the front row of the gathering hall. Everyone was quiet. The village sage stood at the front of the assembly, his hands raised.

His brother lay in front, stretched atop a decorative catafalque and covered in a sheer white shroud. When Phoenix saw him, he could not look away. Lit candles surrounded him, casting an ethereal glow in the gathering hall.

He was still, but he did not look asleep as people say the dead look. Lorien slept fitfully, with limbs akimbo and his hair mussed. Phoenix had slept in the same room with him his whole life and was intimately familiar. Lorien now appeared too pressed…too perfected. They had coiffed his hair in a careful style that made him look older than his scant years. His hands were rigid, placed over his chest in a semblance of rest.

Beside him, his mother made a small, piteous sound. Her shoulders shook lightly as she wept. It wasn't until he saw his mother, tears streaming down her face, that Phoenix felt the gravity of the moment.

His brother, Lorien, was dead. He would never laugh with him again. He would never play. Phoenix would never see Lorien grow into a man. He felt something inside him shift.

Phoenix gasped. His chest felt tight. His hands shook. The attendants handed him an unlit candle, and he could barely keep it upright.

Darius did not accept a candle. He stood, stoic and sad, looking at his son's body. His mouth was a firm line, his body rigid. Phoenix reached for his hand, but he did not take it.

"Let Lorien's light be a light to all of us," the sage recited. "Approach and share the flame of hope."

Cordera had stopped weeping. Her eyes were puffy beneath the veil. She put a hand on Phoenix's shoulder, softly squeezing it. She led Phoenix up to his brother's body, to the candles that stood on stands around him. "Touch your candle to the flame," she whispered, and Phoenix did so. He watched as it winked to life, one flame becoming two.

The flame cast warmth onto his face, a contrast to the cold gathering hall. Phoenix stared into the flame, so much so that the room went dark around it. He imagined he could see an image of Lorien, alive and happy within the dancing flame. It soothed him. He would carry this light with him; Lorien would be a part of him.

Phoenix looked back at his father. He did not approach Lorien or light a candle. He looked at Phoenix with thinly veiled disdain.

Phoenix swallowed and looked away. His father blamed him for Lorien's death; he realized that now. Lorien was gone, and things would never be the same. No candle would ever change that.

He and his mother returned to their seats. Phoenix heard the sage, but did not hear him. He watched the wax from the candles surrounding his brother's body melt and pool onto the stone floor. He gripped the candle tightly and shut his eyes, wishing above anything that he was somewhere else.

♦ ♦ ♦

The next morning, Phoenix awoke to the realization that Lorien wasn't there. The room was still. Lorien did not pounce on his bed, encouraging him to get up. There was silence.

Then he heard muffled crying. He rolled onto his side, and he saw his mother leaning over Lorien's bed. He rubbed sleep from his eyes.

"Mama?"

Cordera wiped her eyes with a handkerchief. She stood and walked over to Phoenix's bed and sat down on the side of it. "Oh Feenie," she said, grief coloring her words. Her hair was in disarray, and she looked as though she hadn't slept. "Your father's gone."

Phoenix blinked, processing what she'd said. "Gone? Where did he go?"

His mother sighed. She touched her hand to his cheek, thumbing away a tear he didn't realize had fallen.

"He left us, baby. We're alone, now."

He closed his eyes. When he opened them, he was in a bright white room. There was the touch of a hand on his face…soft but sure. He looked and Pearla was leaning over him. "You're not alone, love," she was saying to him. Phoenix looked up at her face. He knew it so well…could map every freckle, count every eyelash. "Hi," he breathed, and the smile that lit her face was like a balm to his soul.

Lorien's loss still lingered. His father's absence, gone so many years now, seemed fresh. But they were dreams…ghosts from his past, haunting him here at his lowest physical point. He knew that now.

"I'm worried," Phoenix began, his mouth dry. "I don't think I'm gonna make it, Pearl."

Pearla tutted, her eyes sad. "Oh, Phoenix, don't say that." She held his face in her hands, just like his mother had in his dream. "You're going to be fine. Sev is going to make it back…then we'll have the rest of our lives."

76

Phoenix's mouth turned down. He felt the tears before he realized it and tried to wipe them away.

His arm wouldn't move.

Pearla dabbed at his face with a tissue, being extra gentle. She must've seen the alarm in his eyes, because she reached down and held his hand. He couldn't feel it. His chest became tight, fear threatening to overtake him.

"The doctors said you could experience some paralysis," she informed him. "But it's temporary, Phoenix." He watched her squeeze his hand as if to prove her point. "You're going to be fine."

He wanted to believe her, but the tears came unbidden. Pearla climbed up beside him and simply held him as he grieved. He cried for Lorien…for the father he never really had. And he cried for himself.

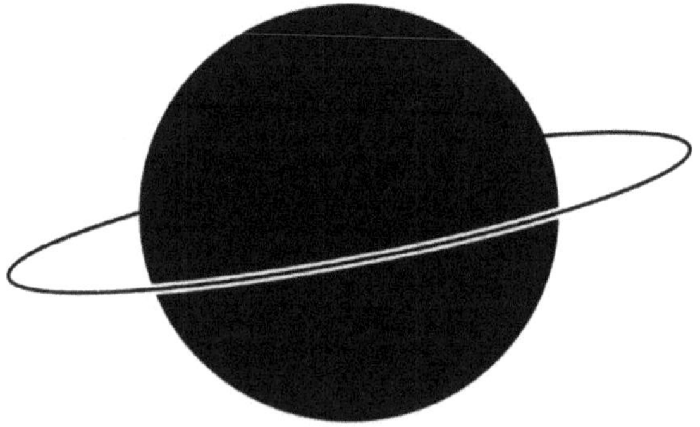

CHAPTER 15

Sev started awake. The rumble and roar of the shipping barge was hard to ignore. She could feel the vibration of the metal beneath her, the cold of space seeping into the cargo hold.

They were in the Black, barreling toward Dobani.

It made her both happy and sad, to know with every breath she took she was closer and closer to her home planet, but further away from her family.

Sev checked her chrono. Hours had passed since she snuck on board. Without a nav screen, she had no way to discern their location, but it didn't matter. They were on the way, and that's what counted.

She tested her limbs. They were stiff with cold and from being folded beneath her. Her arms too, so she stretched catlike in the dark cargo hold, trying to get some of the feeling back and assessing her body. Her ankle was better; she had not re-injured it by jumping onto the barge. That much, at least, was going for her.

Sev's stomach protested, and she frowned. The ration bar Soren had left her (and she believed that now, that he left it specifically for her) was long gone, though the memory of it warmed her.

She stood on shaky legs and looked around. It was dim and dusty in the cargo hold. Large crates took up most of the space. She chose a crate with a loose board and worked her fingers through the cracks. She pulled, splinters cracking and giving way. Something tumbled forth, bouncing on the floor of the cargo hold.

Sev picked it up. She could smell it…a sharp, earthy smell. When she turned it over in her hands, she smiled.

It was a purple tuber. Her favorite back home.

She scrubbed the dirt off it and took a bite. The bitter sweetness flooded her mouth, making her stomach growl again. She ate heartily, hungrier than she thought. Sev had nearly finished the whole thing when she heard a noise, something bumping into a crate.

She stopped, straining her ears to discern the sound. There was nothing but the noise of the shipping barge, the hum of space.

"Never thought to break into one," a voice came from the darkness, and Sev thrust her hand out in front of her, immediately assuming a defensive posture. She still held the tuber.

A girl stepped out of the shadows. She appeared a little older than Sev and had her hands up. "I'm not going to hurt you," she said as she took a slow step forward. "I'm just hungry. That's all."

She was Ocarri, that much Sev could tell. Her pale skin and black eyes were the same as Soren's. She had long, wavy hair that reached past her shoulders. Unlike Sev, she appeared fully equipped for the cold.

And she looked just as scared as Sev was.

"What's your name?" Sev asked her. "What are you doing here?"

The girl's mouth quirked in some semblance of a smile. "Same as you, I imagine." She stuck out her hand. "Name's Mira."

Sev looked at her hand, but did not take it.

Mira smiled, her eyes up in question. "You gonna hit me with that potato, or are we going to handle this like friends?"

Sev lowered her makeshift weapon, still a little wary. "It's a tuber," she told her. "And I'm not your friend." In her brief experience on Ocarro, she'd only met one Ocarri that wasn't trying to harm, delay, or detain her, and that was Soren. Sev sat back down behind the crate, folding her arms over her chest.

Mira straightened. She still had a slight smile on her face. "Can I have one?"

Sev jerked her head toward the open crate, refusing to look at her. "Plenty for both of us," she said, her voice terse.

The girl grinned. "Thanks a lot," she said. Sev watched her walk to the open crate and pull out a tuber. She bit into it, dirt and all.

Sev grimaced. The girl ate with voracity, sitting there against the crate not very far from Sev. Sev wondered when her last meal was.

Mira was most of the way through her second tuber when she finally slowed down to a normal pace. She looked at Sev, her lips stained purple. "You're an off-worlder. Why are you on Ocarro, anyway?"

Sev raised her head to look at her. Mira looked less threatening with her mouthful of purple tubers. She took a breath. "My father is sick," she said. "They couldn't help him on Dobani." She looked down briefly, glancing at where her hands lay crossed in her lap. "It was my idea to come here, and now things are worse."

Mira nodded. She'd finished eating and seemed content. "That's how they get you here. That famous Ocarri medicine." She rolled her eyes, her mouth firm. "But there's always a catch."

Sev frowned. "I found that out," she said, her voice full of regret. "What about you? Why are you leaving your home?"

Mira appeared somber. "I tested into engineering. High marks. The government mandates that I enter the program soon, but that's not what I want to do." Her eyes grew bright. "I want to be a teacher."

Sev smiled. "My father is in school to be a teacher. He's going to be a good one, too. He's caring. Compassionate. Patient. The smartest person I know. He was born to be a teacher."

Mira inclined her head. "You really love him, don't you?"

Tears filled her eyes. Sev smiled. "With everything I have."

Sev looked at her, considering. "My name's Sev." She stuck out her hand across the space between them, and Mira took it.

She smiled. "Nice to meet you, Sev."

Sev cleared her throat. "I'm sorry I was rude before. You just scared me, is all."

Mira shrugged. "No worries," she said pleasantly. "Say, do you know where we're going?"

Sev chuckled. "We're going to my home planet. Dobani. So, you just climbed on the first transport you saw, huh?"

Mira drew one knee up to her chest, resting her arm on it. "Yep. All I knew was it was outbound. It was worth the risk just to get off this ball of ice."

Sev laughed. "Well, you'll love Dobani. It's warm most of the time. With a beautiful ocean. The people are welcoming to off-worlders. I wasn't born there, yet it's home to me now. And on Dobani, you can be whatever you like."

Mira was listening intently, her eyes wide. "Sounds amazing."

Sev smiled. She thought of her father, how he loved the life they had there. How, years ago, when they'd arrived injured and exhausted straight from the Black, he had never pressured her to move on. They'd simply stayed for a time. They'd healed. And that time turned into months, and those months into years, and neither of them had regretted it.

She looked away briefly, lost in the memories. "It is," she said. "And I think you'll make a wonderful teacher."

Mira smiled. Neither of them said anything for a long time. Sev dozed, full of tubers and exhausted from her journey. Sometime later, the barge shook as they broke atmosphere, the metal walls of the ship heating red hot. Shipping barges didn't have the insulation that passenger transports had. People were never supposed to be in these cargo holds, so the shipbuilders didn't bother.

Sev and Mira sat on a crate, the metal floor of the ship too hot to touch. With no safety straps, they wrapped themselves in the cargo nets that held the crates. Mira looked at Sev, fear in her dark eyes.

"What's happening?"

Sev looked at her, her eyes soft. Mira must've never left the planet, as unused to space travel as she was, she thought. "We're breaking atmosphere. It's the roughest part of any journey. Just hold on, Mira. We'll be on Dobani soon."

Mira shut her eyes tight. She said something in Ocarri, something low and urgent. A prayer, maybe, for safety. For strength. Sev gripped the cargo net until her fingers were white, bracing herself.

◆ ◆ ◆

The landing was not the worst she'd experienced, but it had shaken Mira to the core. They waited until the repulsor lifts had carried the shipping barge into a warehouse for unloading, then made their move. When the hatch was open, Mira and Sev snuck out behind a gravsled full of crates, making it outside the warehouse and into the bright Dobani sun.

They were in the business district. Sev remembered it from those long days on the docks with Phoenix. Mira stared, starry-eyed at the bright blue sky, the balmy wind that came in off the water.

For a moment, they stood facing each other, neither of them ready to say goodbye. Sev moved first, hugging her. Mira returned it, placing her head on her shoulder. She sighed. "Thank you for being my friend," Mira said to her, "even if you said you wouldn't."

Sev huffed a laugh. She withdrew and reached into the pocket of the coat that was feeling overly warm now. She pulled out a punch card.

"There's enough on here to get you settled. For you to get in school."

Mira took it, tears in her dark eyes. "Thank you, Sev." She hugged her again, and Sev let her. "I hope you get back to your dad real soon," she whispered. "I know he misses you."

Sev nodded. She patted Mira on the shoulder and turned, leaving her there outside the warehouse with a hopeful expression on her face.

"Good luck," she said over her shoulder. Mira held her up her hand, the pinky finger pointing skyward. "On Ocarro, this means 'my heart goes with you'," she said. "Good luck to you, Sev."

Sev smiled. Mira was very much like she was once. Landing on Dobani and looking for a fresh start. She hoped it would turn out just as good as it did for her.

She turned down the familiar streets, headed towards home.

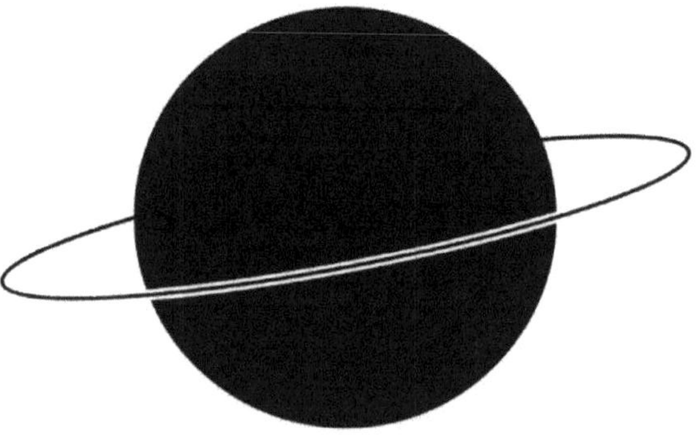

CHAPTER 16

Just inside Dobani Proper, Sev hailed a transport. She had shed the coat in the balmy Dobani weather, and it lay on the seat beside her. She thought of Mira, of how their paths had crossed in the unlikeliest of ways. Something told her that Mira would be happy here.

She was contemplative most of the journey home; the driver did not chat, and she was thankful. She had so much to do that it was almost overwhelming. Her mind buzzed with thoughts.

The transport turned down the sandy driveway. In the distance, their palm grove stood proud and strong, and to the left, their little house.

Her heart twinged at the sight of it, sitting serenely by the Dobani Sea. Not much had changed in the years since they moved in; their little house had always had good bones, and beyond the predictable cosmetic fixes, she and Phoenix didn't have to do much to it.

She paid the driver and turned up the path to the front door. The tracks of the medical transport remained pressed in the sandy yard, rigid and distinct. She swallowed. She remembered it like it was yesterday.

Her key slid in the lock with a satisfying snick, and she turned the handle. The door opened to a dark house. Dust motes stirred in the mostly stale air; the house had lain dormant for as many days as they'd been on Ocarro.

At her feet were her and Pearla's packages. They'd gone shopping that morning.

Sev picked one up and turned it over in her hands. It was a medium-sized box tied with string. Her dress, she thought. Her eyes stung. She never got the chance to ask him, and now it was too late.

Sev dropped the package along with the others and stepped past them.

She flipped on the living room lamp. The new light showed a life interrupted; Phoenix's stim cup on the end table, long cold now. His slippers at the end of the couch. There were a few throw pillows on the floor, probably knocked off when the medics came to move him.

Sev looked over at the mantle. Her adoption papers still hung proudly, albeit a little dusty, for all to see. Her mouth turned up in a smile. She remembered the night she'd given them to him…they'd barely had furniture, then. Everything was so new…their life together was so fragile.

She felt morose, like a dark cloud hung over her and she couldn't shake it. Sev wandered into the kitchen. If she closed her eyes, she could see Phoenix standing at the counter, humming those old songs, or Pearla sitting by the window, drinking her stim brew. They weren't there, though. It was just her…alone in this house that suddenly seemed much larger than it was.

Sev shook her head. She couldn't do this, she reminded herself. Her father needed her. Pearla needed her. There was much to do before going to Terra Firma. She needed a suit, for one, and since they hadn't manufactured them since the Council of Planets had banned Terra Firma, getting one would be no small feat.

But she had an idea.

◆ ◆ ◆

The junkyard was much like she remembered, although it'd been years since she'd been here. Old ships, carbon condensers, and various scrapped engines lined the pathway to the middle of the complex. She followed the trail, hearing him first before seeing him.

"Stars alive, this confounded machine," came a grumbling voice, followed by a crash and an exclamation of pain. He stood, rubbing the top of his head, and slammed the hatch shut. He saw her, and it took a moment for him to register who it was.

"Sev? That you?" He waddled forward, his dirty white t-shirt riding up over his belly. He held a wrench in his hand, and he promptly tossed it onto the pile, along with other assorted tools.

Sev smiled, walking forward with her hands in her pockets. "Hey Uncle Dak. It's good to see you."

Dak grunted, still rubbing his head. He pulled a handkerchief out of his pocket and started wiping his hands free of grease and dirt. "What brings you here, little lady? I haven't seen you in a moon's age."

Sev ducked her head, gathering resolve. When she looked up, there was conviction in her eyes. "Kinda need a favor, Dak."

Dak frowned. He sat on a metal drum nearby and offered one to Sev. "Since when do you and Phoenix not come around here wantin' somethin'?" he grumbled. "Where is that old buzzard, anyway?"

Sev looked away before answering. "He's on Ocarro. He's sick, Dak. I need spores from Terra Firma to—"

"Whoa now, little lady. Ocarro? What in blazes—" he shook his head, letting the news register. "What is he doing on Ocarro? That blasted ball of ice…"

Sev folded her arms over her chest. "Dobani doctors didn't know what was wrong with him. So, we went to Ocarro. And they can cure him, Dak. But I need to go back to Terra Firma."

Dak stood, his knees creaking with the motion. "Got no business on Terra Firma. You never did. Being a little girl and all that." He snorted, looking down at the ground. "Get yourself killed, that's what you'll do."

Sev stood, meeting him. "Not a little girl anymore, Dak. I can handle myself. I always could."

He looked down before meeting her eyes. He was on the fence, she could tell. It was very possible he might not help her. And if that happened, she didn't know what she would do.

"Dak," Sev implored. "He's going to die. He'll die if I don't get the spores. I *have* to go back."

Dak snorted. He brushed his sparse hair away from his forehead. The motion reminded her of Phoenix. "It's illegal," he said.

Sev smiled. "That's never stopped you before."

He huffed. Sev held his gaze, unflinching. She could tell he saw it now. Her resolve.

She was going with or without his help, and he knew it. Somehow, she would find a way. And maybe, just maybe, helping her was the only way he could help Phoenix.

"Tell me what you need," he said, relenting, and Sev wrapped him in a big hug.

◆ ◆ ◆

They talked well into the night. Dak's home was close and cluttered, but clean. He'd served them root juice straight from the bottle, but Sev nursed hers while Dak drank heartily. They reminisced, mostly, about Sev and Phoenix fixing up the skiff all those years ago. About the parts Dak had bartered for on the black market.

Dak leaned forward, his hands on his knees. "So, you need a suit. By Drek, you might as well want the moon, little lady. Those things are hard to find."

Sev quirked her mouth. "If I know anything about you, it's that you're a master of the 'hard to find'."

Dak took a sip of his drink. "Aye, I do have a knack," he agreed. "But it'll cost you."

Sev narrowed her eyes. Perhaps Dak's affection for her and Phoenix did not go as far as she had hoped. She braced herself, wondering what his price would be.

"Two pieces of that shiny stuff," Dak said, his eyes a little starry. "Two perfect pieces of calcet, and we'll call it a deal."

Sev considered. No one had been to Terra Firma in years. She wasn't sure there were any jewels left there.

She finally nodded, sticking out her hand. "Deal. I'll get you your calcet. I promise."

Dak smiled, tipping his bottle before taking Sev's hand in agreement.

◆ ◆ ◆

It was after midnight when she returned home. It was strange, getting in after the tide. Her father wouldn't approve, but given how much affection he had for Uncle Dak, he might make an exception.

Sev showered and changed before slipping beneath the covers. She watched the moon as it hung low over the water, full and bright. The house was still…unnaturally quiet. She thought of Phoenix, lost somewhere in his sickness on Ocarro…somewhere she couldn't reach him.

I'm coming, Daddy, she thought to herself. *Wait for me. I'm coming.*

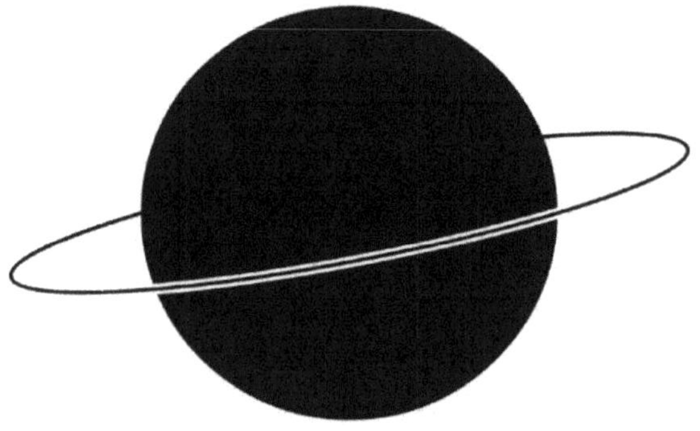

CHAPTER 17

The spade dug into the hard earth, kicking up dirt and rocks. The dust from the ground was overwhelming; it coated his skin, a fine sheen of brown dust that spoke of a cruel dry season…of withered crops and empty stomachs.

"Hurry now, Feenie. We've only got a handful of potatoes for our stew tonight. Help me get these last few and we'll be eating well!"

But Phoenix knew there would be no stew. He followed his mother down the rows, digging up small, shriveled potatoes she'd later boil alongside bitter herbs. The stew she spoke of was more like soup, but she would season it with what she had, making it flavorful. It would be hot and would stop the hunger pangs until morning.

She kept what they dug up in the pocket of her faded apron. His mother had aged in the years since their father left. Gray streaked her hair, and the sun had weathered her skin from working the fields. But she still had the same kind smile, the same delicate touch, and the same sadness in her eyes.

That night, Cordera didn't eat. She sat at the table with Phoenix, mending his pants.

"Eat, Mama," Phoenix encouraged her. But he looked in the pot, and there was none left. The potatoes had only made enough for him.

Cordera smiled softly. "I'm fine, dear heart. You go on now. You've got to grow big and strong. I'm all done growing."

The stew soured in his stomach. He pushed his plate away, even though he had over half left and was still hungry. "I want you to have it," he said as he nudged it in her direction. His eyes grew bright as he looked up at her. "We can share," he said with a hopeful smile. "Like me and Lorien used to."

A shadow passed over her face, and he immediately regretted the words. She took the bowl with tender hands and raised the spoon to her lips. "Ok baby," she relented. "Like you and Lori used to."

The night grew cold. There was no wood for fire, no oil for the lamps. Cordera sat by the dark fireplace, wrapped in a quilt. Her teeth were chattering.

Phoenix came in with his arms full of books. "Burn these, Mama. I've already read them. It's ok."

Cordera looked at her son with tears in her eyes. She clutched him in a fierce hug, rocking him back and forth. "Drek knows I never wanted this for you, baby," she whispered. "I wanted better. I still want better."

Phoenix kissed his mother's cheek. "I'll get the matches, Mama. We'll be warm tonight. Don't cry."

Phoenix placed his beloved books in the fireplace and lit a match. The books caught fast, blackened pages curling and flying away, drifting toward the flue. They slept there, curled up by the fire. It was the warmest night they'd spent.

The next morning, there was a heavy frost. Cordera made porridge with the last of the oats. There was enough for both, and the hot mash warmed their stomachs and lifted their spirits.

Phoenix watched as his mother took the quilt from the back of the couch. It was her grandmother's, hand-sewn over long months. He had always admired it, tracing the intricate patterns with his fingers as a child.

Now he saw the way her hands lingered over the fabric, the way her thumb smoothed over the intricate edges, her expression unreadable.

Then it hit him.

She wasn't admiring it. She was weighing its worth.

Grief settled in his chest. His mother was thinking of what it would fetch at market.

After another pass of her hand over the material, she had decided.

Without a word, Cordera turned and walked away, leaving Phoenix standing by the fireplace, long gone cold.

Tonight, they would eat meat. They would not starve. And with whatever money remained, she would buy seeds for the spring.

Phoenix watched her go, helpless to stop her. She looked so small walking down the dusty driveway, the grass on either side covered in frost. Her dress was thin, her coat threadbare. His mother deserved better.

He would provide one day, he swore to himself, even if it was the last thing he did. He would not see his mother picked apart by poverty piece by piece.

♦ ♦ ♦

The doctor walked into Phoenix's room, and he started awake. Phoenix still could not move…could not feel his limbs. He almost preferred being haunted by dreams of the past rather than suffering the reality of being paralyzed, of seeing Pearla cry and being unable to wipe her tears.

"Good morning, Mr. Phoenix. My name is Prescott. I'll be taking over your care."

Pearla straightened, her hand on Phoenix's arm. "What happened to Soren?"

Prescott's mouth softened into a slight frown. "Unfortunately, Soren is being imprisoned for helping Sev escape. He no longer works here."

Pearla's eyes widened, and her hand flew to her mouth. "We've got to help him," she exclaimed.

Prescott only nodded. "I'm working on that," he said. "For right now, I'm focused on you, Phoenix. How are you feeling?"

Phoenix grew quiet. "I'm having dreams," he said. "Very vivid dreams. Of the past, mostly."

Prescott hummed. "Common with Lumiers. I'm afraid it's a side effect of our medicine here. Any other complaints?"

Phoenix closed his eyes. When he opened them, they had misted with tears. "Why can't I feel my legs, Doc? My arm?" His voice shook with emotion, and Pearla gripped his hand, though he couldn't feel it.

The doctor inclined his head. "It's the treatment. The Lumiers immobilizes you as it's clearing your body of infection. It's only temporary."

Pearla looked up at Prescott; her tired eyes had dark circles under them. "How long?"

Prescott crossed his arms. "Eighteen months. Maybe a year."

Phoenix gasped, and Pearla made a startled sound. "I can't waste away here a year, Doc," Phoenix told him gravely. "It's not in nature. I'm not a sedentary man. I've got school, and Sev. Got to be about my life now. Surely you understand."

The doctor looked sympathetic. "I do," he said. "And maybe it won't be that long. Maybe there are other ways. But for now, I think you need to rest. Pearla? May I see you for a moment?"

Phoenix watched them leave. The door snicked shut behind them, loud in the cavernous room.

Prescott led Pearla to the waiting room. The antiseptic smell of the hospital lingered here, too, along with the smell of stale stim and the earthy wet smell of potted plants. She sat down, and he sat across from her.

"Pearla, do you have somewhere to stay? Where have you been sleeping?"

She looked down, abashed. "In here, mostly. Or beside Phoenix." She looked up as if he was going to make her go. "I don't want to leave him."

He smiled. "I'm not saying you have to. But you need to take better care of yourself. For Phoenix, too."

He reached into his pocket and withdrew a card with a room number on it. "There's a support group for family members that meets here twice a week. It's just down the hall. I think the group would really love to meet you, Pearla." He patted her arm. "You might even like it, too."

Pearla took the card and tucked it away. She doubted she would ever need it, but she appreciated the gesture all the same. She looked up at the doctor with tearful eyes. "Now that Soren is gone, there'll be no serum, will there?"

Prescott dropped his head. "Pearla, it's likely Sev won't make it back. That's something you need to prepare for. Prepare Phoenix for. That's why I think the support group might be a good idea."

Pearla turned away from him, not wanting to hear it. If Soren was gone, Sev was risking her life for nothing. Prescott stood and walked toward the door of the waiting room. "That card also has my private number. Use it, Pearla, if you ever need anything."

She watched him walk out. The card burned in her pocket, but she had never felt more alone.

CHAPTER 18

The mess hall was noisy with the grumblings of over a hundred inmates, plus whatever organizational system it took to serve food to so many people three times a day.

Soren guessed it was food. Looking at his tin tray, he wasn't so sure.

Brown globulous chunks floated in an unfamiliar gravy. A white mound of what he could only guess was some sort of starch sat off to the side, monolithic and unappetizing. Topping it off, a cup of what looked like fruit sat in one of the little dividers. He picked it up, tested it with his spoon, and took a bite.

Cyrus must've seen the disagreeable look on his face, because he chuckled. "You'll get used to it. The protein mash isn't that bad. Keeps you strong."

Soren appraised him with doubt, seeing as Cyrus was feeble and in poor health.

Still, the fruit wasn't terrible…not quite ripe, but not offensive.

Cyrus pointed his spoon at him. He was wearing his eyepatch, as he did whenever he associated with the general population. He claimed it made him look tough, to which Soren had only smiled.

"You'll need to eat eventually, and more than fruit. Especially when they put you on a work detail."

Soren said nothing. He figured, with the severity of his crimes, that he would never live to see a work detail. They would bring him before the council soon enough, and they would sentence him to death.

It did not scare him like he thought it might.

Soren put down the fruit cup, his appetite gone. "You got anybody on the outside, Cyrus? Family?" He grinned. "A woman?"

Cyrus scowled. "Nobody to speak of," he said, and he grew quiet for a moment. "Not since my son."

Soren nodded. He looked up to see a guard approaching their table. The man motioned to him.

"You've got a visitor, 227. You can follow me."

Cyrus laughed, then it trailed off into an ugly cough. "Must be someone important to pull you away from this fine meal," he said, catching his breath.

Soren quirked his mouth in an aborted smile and stood to follow the guard from the mess hall.

The man kept his hand on his arm, leading him to the visitor's center. There was nowhere for Soren to go, though…to Soren, it seemed like overkill.

They traversed the dank halls, overhead lights buzzing loudly until they arrived in front of the door to the visitor's center. Inside was a large room with multiple tables, allowing families and friends to visit with the incarcerated. Soren had neither, so he wondered who could be here to see him.

The guard led him through the door, and he searched the room until he found him sitting alone at a table by the barred window. Prescott.

Soren smiled genuinely for the first time in a long time. The guard walked him over and pushed him down onto the bench seat across from Prescott, cuffing his hands to a metal ring in the middle of the table.

Prescott looked up, visibly surprised. "Is that really necessary?"

The guard shrugged. "It's protocol." He looked at Soren sternly. "You have fifteen minutes."

Soren met his gaze and saw the way Prescott's eyes flickered over him, taking in the weight he'd lost, the dullness in his reflection, the gray pallor of his skin. The pity there was unmistakable. Soren clenched his bound hands, frustrated, and Prescott's gaze dropped to them. The older man licked his lips, hesitating before speaking.

"I've taken over Phoenix's care. I wanted you to know that."

Hope soared in Soren's heart. "So, you'll make the serum?"

Prescott looked away. "The treatment is Lumiers. We've already started."

Soren pounded the metal table with his shackled fist. "You know that's not enough, Prescott. It's not going to work."

Prescott swallowed. "Lumiers has a very high success rate. If we just trust the process—"

"Don't recite Ocarri medical propaganda to me, Prescott. It's insulting. Not after everything we've been through."

Prescott hesitated, and Soren could see the shift in his expression—the recognition, the memory. He knew what Prescott saw: not the prisoner before him, but the grieving young man he'd met years ago. Soren could feel the weight of that past pressing between them. He still had the same unruly hair, the same eyes Prescott had once called kind. Back then, his heart had been set on healing, though it had come with a rebellious streak that ran in contrast to Ocarri medicine. He smiled to himself. Some things never changed.

"Saving Phoenix won't bring back your mother, Soren." Prescott lowered his head, almost hesitant to say it. "It won't change anything."

Soren looked up at him. There was a fire in his eyes that wasn't there before. "For Sev, it will change *everything*. You must do this, Prescott. If not for Phoenix, then do it for me."

Prescott looked away, through the window, unable to meet his eyes. "It's against the rules," he argued weakly.

Soren scoffed. "And you've never broken rules? Who encouraged me to go into medicine in the first place, Prescott? Hmm?"

Prescott relented. He became sober. "You know what might happen to you, don't you?"

Soren swallowed. "They're going to kill me," he said matter-of-factly.

It made Prescott flinch to hear it aloud. Tears filled Prescott's eyes. "I took you in like a son. Mentored you. Taught you everything I know."

Soren smiled. "Then help me save a life…this one last time."

Soren watched the hesitation flicker across Prescott's face. He was considering it. Soren could see it in the way his jaw tightened, the way his fingers twitched, as if grasping at the consequences. It was against protocol. Risking his career, his reputation, everything he'd built. And if this plan failed…

But there was something else in his expression, something Soren had never been sure of before. A sense of responsibility. Maybe even guilt. Prescott had once shaped him, guided him into medicine, molded him into a younger version of himself—before Ocarri bureaucracy had beaten the fight out of him.

Soren swallowed hard. If there was anything left of that man, the one who had believed in him, maybe there was hope.

He watched as Prescott looked down at his shackled hands; he was weighing the gravity of the moment, he knew. Realizing how much Soren had already lost.

"You better hope Sev makes it back," he said.

Soren smiled, relieved. "She'll make it back."

The guard interrupted them, telling Soren his time was up. He led him away, his hands and feet still shackled. Soren looked back over his shoulder. Prescott held his hand up in an Ocarri farewell, one pinky pointing toward the sky. "I'll do what I can," he promised.

For Soren, it would have to be enough.

◆ ◆ ◆

Chow time was over, so they led him back to his cell. Cyrus was on his bunk, his hands crossed over his chest, his eyepatch off so that his milk-glass eye shown in the near dark. Going from the large space to such a small one made Soren feel suffocated and a little helpless.

He sat down on his bunk, his feet over the edge. Cyrus looked at him critically. "How was the visit?" he groused.

Soren sighed, his head down. "I don't know yet," he said. "I hope, good."

Cyrus turned on his cot, the old springs creaking with the movement. "Fair enough," he said to no one. "But hope is a dangerous thing."

Soren sat with his back against the cool concrete. It grounded him. Hope was dangerous, but necessary. He had to have faith that Prescott would follow his heart and not his head.

CHAPTER 19

They said nothing on the way. It was raining, and fat droplets pelted the view pane of Dak's beat-up transport, blurring the focus of the world outside. Sev saw the outline of the skiff in the distance, standing bright and blue against the stormy sky. It was just as she remembered.

"I haven't been to the landing pad in years now," she said wistfully. "You think the skiff is ready to go?"

Dak gave her his best approximation of a smile. "Me and the boys kept it up," he grunted. "Least we could do for what we owe Phoenix."

Sev smiled. Her father was a generous man, always had been. She didn't doubt he had shared his half of the calcet wealth with his friends, though he never said as much.

Dak pulled up to the landing pad and parked in the shadow cast by the skiff. The rain had stopped. It wasn't a large ship, but Sev preferred the smaller size. Easy to handle. Easier to maintain. The sun came out, gleaming on the potbellied hull.

Dak climbed out of the transport and reached for his toolkit. He took something out, pocketed it, and walked toward the skiff. Sev followed.

They stood at the ramp leading to the hatch. The air was hazy as it was after a rainstorm in the warmer months. She breathed in the heady scent of the wet ground, taking a deep breath.

She may never see this again.

It weighed heavily on her, now, the gravity of what she was about to do. There were never any guarantees about going to Terra Firma. No promise that she would return. The risk was significant…she was keenly aware of it now, more than ever.

"Thanks for bringing me, Uncle Dak. And for everything."

She had her suit in her pack. He traded for it used, but in good condition…a rare find in this post Terra Firma world. The other supplies she'd asked for were that as well. She had all she needed…now if luck and the cosmos would cooperate, she would be successful.

Dak sniffed. "Phoenix would have my hide if I let his little girl go off to Terra Firma alone," he said not unfondly. "Least I could do."

She hugged him. He stood there a little rigid at first, then he finally returned it. "Be careful, Sev," he whispered. "Terra Firma has sat in the wild for years now. It's not the planet you remember."

She withdrew. He appeared serious and uncharacteristically worried.

"Watch yourself."

She nodded. He reached into his pocket and withdrew a small headlamp. She recognized it as the one he'd been wearing when she walked up on him in the junkyard.

"Take this. Use it." He smiled then, lopsided and fond. "Who knows, it may get you out of a jam."

Sev took the headlamp gingerly and put it away. "Thank you so much. And I will."

She turned to walk up the ramp to the ship's hatch. Dak watched her go…stood there until the thrusters ignited and the skiff took off into the rain-soaked sky. When he finally drove away, he did not look back.

♦ ♦ ♦

Being at the controls again felt surreal. She missed her father, his solid presence beside her. When the gray sky of Dobani had bled into the thick black canvas of space, Sev sat back and looked out of the view pane at the infinite landscape of stars and thought of home.

Not Dobani or even their little house. She thought of her father…of Pearla. Because Sev had learned a long time ago that home was more than just a place. It was the people who loved you.

She looked at the hatch…she had been in such a rush to get going, to get the ship off the ground that she had missed their handprints pressed by the door…the handprints they'd made so many years ago, when the skiff was newly theirs and their relationship was in its infancy. She stood and traced her finger over the print before pressing her hand to it.

Her hand used to be so much smaller than his, she marveled. Now hers nearly matched. She looked down at the handprint beneath his, child-sized but sure. An unnamed emotion welled within her. They'd been through so much.

Sev backed away and sat down in the navigator's chair, her usual seat when alongside her father. A tear rolled down her cheek, then another. Her chest grew tight, and she felt the sob before it erupted, loud and broken in the small space.

Sev let herself cry. This was the first time since his illness that she had indulged in actual tears without trying to conceal or stifle them. Her shoulders shook…her breath came in little hitches, tears streaming down her face. It was cleansing. It was a much-needed release.

With the ship safely on autopilot, Sev reclined in the chair and closed her eyes, exhausted.

Sometime later, a proximity alarm sounded. She jolted from sleep, eyes on the scanners. Something had crossed into her flight path. Something big.

Getting around it would require a burn of the thrusters, essentially equal to dumping fuel into space. She made the mental calculations. She could afford one burn and maybe one on the way back, if there was an emergency. Sev held her hand over the switch that would divert their course. *Every burn counts, little mouse*, she heard her father say. Sev took a breath and initiated the change.

If she was off by a meter, she was cooked. If she was off by more than that, she would spin off into the Black, out of control and off course.

The thrusters roared. Fire shot out from the ship, canting it slightly. Sev strapped herself in and hoped it would be enough (but not too much).

After a few tense moments, the ship grew still. Sev directed it back on course, safely around the object. Whether it was a passing meteor or space junk, she couldn't tell.

She thought of Terra Firma, of Uncle Dak's words of advice. Terra Firma had lain undisturbed for years, untouched by man. There was no telling what lay in wait for her.

But Sev was confident. She'd been twice…knew her way around. After all, Terra Firma couldn't have changed that much, could it?

She unpacked, laying out her suit. Uncle Dak was lucky to have found one, and in such good condition, too. The filter was sound, if not brand new.

Sev ran her hands over her supplies, taking care that she had everything she needed. Hydration packs, nutrition. Tools for the spore retrieval.

And a weapon. Her hand hovered over the air gun she'd taken from her father's room on Dobani, hesitant to touch it. She thought of how destructive they were; Del had died from an air gun injury, and Phoenix gravely injured. She didn't want to have to use it, but if she had to, she would.

Just in case, she thought.

CHAPTER 20

Pearla looked at Phoenix where he slept. The treatment was exhausting him, causing him vivid dreams that he had a hard time waking up from. She stood, stretching. Her back ached from that stiff chair; her stomach rumbled. It was probably time to visit the nutrition station, though she had no appetite.

She took a sip of her stim, recoiling at the cool, bitter liquid. It had grown cold and stale, and if there was something she couldn't abide, it was cold stim.

Pearla ducked into the facilities and poured the drink down the sink. She looked up, catching herself in the mirror.

She was barely recognizable.

Pearla traced the dark circles under her eyes, her disheveled hair. Her skin had grown pale and sallow while locked away from the sun. Her face was thin.

She looked down at her empty cup. She felt jittery, exhausted. But she had to keep going. Her reflection stared back at her, and beyond the tiredness, she saw the resolve there. The determination. She would not give up. She couldn't. Phoenix needed her. So did Sev.

She exited the bathroom and headed out into the hall. There was fresh stim brew in the waiting room. She could visit the nutrition station while she was there.

Pearl made her way down the hall. It was busier than usual in the Medical Center. Doctors and medics passed her in the hall, often with a courteous nod or sometimes a short greeting. Pearla heard unfamiliar voices floating from a room up ahead. Then, most curious of all, laughing.

Laughing was not something she was used to hearing here, where most people were suffering or near death. Her curiosity piqued, she stopped in the doorway. The room was open.

"Hi!" came a chipper voice. It belonged to a woman with a pleasant smile. She motioned her in.

Pearla flushed. She tried to back away, to keep walking, but she'd already aroused attention. "Hi," she replied shyly, her hand up in an aborted wave.

The woman who'd spoken was walking towards her. Pearla looked past her, further into the room. There were people in chairs arranged in a circle. Prescott was sitting in the middle.

She smiled at him, happy to see a familiar face. The woman took Pearla by the arm and led her inside. "I'm so glad you could join us," she enthused. "We've been looking for new members."

The woman led Pearla to an empty chair. Prescott smiled at her a little apologetically, as if understanding she had become an unwilling victim of the women's enthusiasm. "Welcome, Pearla."

The people in the circle all said hello, nearly in unison. Some were Ocarri, others were off-worlders. Given the diversity of the group, Perala didn't feel too out of place.

"So, getting back to our topic of discussion," Prescott continued. "What have you found that you miss the most of your life before illness? What is something you wish you could still do?"

The group looked contemplative. One person shifted and raised her hand, a woman with light blue skin.

"I miss cooking for my family…all of us around the table for a meal. With Rafe as sick as he is, we are no longer together. He's here. Stuck. And so am I."

The woman dotted her eyes with a napkin, and someone patted her on the shoulder. Prescott looked somber, but attentive.

"That's understandable, Drella. It's so hard on the entire family unit when one of them gets sick." He looked around the circle. "Would anyone else like to share?"

The desire to speak burned within her, but Pearla said nothing. She stared down at her stim cup. It was full and fresh; someone had replaced it without her looking. She looked to her left, and the woman that had welcomed her in smiled at her. "Go on," she encouraged. "We're all here for the same thing."

Pearla took a breath. "Um, it sounds selfish…and I really don't mean it to be. But I miss my shop. I'm a shopkeeper on Dobani. I miss my customers. The people I work with." She looked down at the stim, tightening her hand around the cup. "Does that make me a bad person?"

"Oh no, hon," another woman assured her. "We all miss our old lives, the people we were before we were caretakers. We honor that by taking care of ourselves, too. That's important, especially for you, with the baby."

Pearla inhaled sharply. *The baby?* But she wasn't pregnant; she was certain. The timing was off, and besides, she had never even thought of having children. *Would Phoenix even want another child?*

She looked at Prescott. He gave her a knowing smile before addressing the circle. "I think that's all for today," he said. "Thank you all for sharing. Please take some refreshments before you go."

Pearla stood, shaken. Someone led her to the refreshment table and began fixing her a plate piled high with sweets. She tried to refuse.

The woman only smiled. "You look peckish, dear. Let me take care of you."

Pearla accepted the plate with grace, although it was more than she could eat. She pinched off the corner of a sweet roll and chewed it gratefully. She hadn't had fresh food in days; the nutrition station kept her going, but it was far from pleasurable.

She felt a presence behind her. It was Prescott. "Could you meet me in my office, Pearla? After you're finished, of course."

She nodded, balancing her plate in her hands and nodding at the polite conversation from various group members eager to meet her.

◆ ◆ ◆

Pearla knocked on Prescott's door sometime later and he heralded her in. She sat opposite him, ringing her hands nervously.

"Is Phoenix worse?" she asked timidly, afraid of the answer.

Prescott smiled. "No, Pearla. He is stable for now. This is about you."

Pearla paled. "In what way?"

He folded his hands in front of him. "In the way you joined our meeting earlier. Did you enjoy it?"

Pearla smiled. "Everyone's so nice," she mused. "Very welcoming."

Prescott nodded. "We try to be, yes." He pressed a finger to his lips. "I think it would do you some good if you continued with us. At least once a week."

Pearla nodded. "I'll think about it," she said.

He looked at her curiously. "Is that the only thing you're thinking about?"

She studied him, not truly understanding.

"You don't believe what Maris said to you earlier? About you being pregnant?"

Pearla huffed a laugh. "No, it's not my time. Can't be possible."

Prescott suppressed a smile. "That so? Then you wouldn't mind if I scanned you quickly. No reason to get undressed, nothing like that. Just a quick, painless scan."

She considered. Perhaps it was best to put this to rest so she could focus on helping Phoenix recover. And maybe to make herself feel better, too.

"Um, sure," she said. "What do I do?"

Prescott withdrew an instrument from his desk drawer and held it up. It was a device of some type.

"This scans your heartbeat. If there are two, it will pick it up. Are you ready?"

Pearla nodded. Prescott stood, passed the scanner over her, head to toe where she sat. She held her breath, though she was not required to.

"There," he said. "Now we'll play it back and see what we have."

She waited, only a little nervous at what he found.

The device came on in a staticky roar. Prescott adjusted the volume, then made a few more tweaks to the settings. Her heartbeat became audible, a steady sound in the quiet room.

She breathed a sigh of relief. *No baby.*

Then, a thready, rapid beat, much faster than her own. The rhythm thumped alongside hers, steady and strong.

Stars alive.

Prescott smiled and turned off the scanner. "You're pregnant, Pearla. Can't tell how far along without a visual scan, but I'd say a few weeks." He leaned against the edge of the desk, his arms crossed in front of him. "Congratulations."

She looked up at him, a little dumbstruck. *A baby. A new life.* She was going to be a mother.

"Thank you," she said automatically, though she didn't feel very grateful.

Instead, she was terrified.

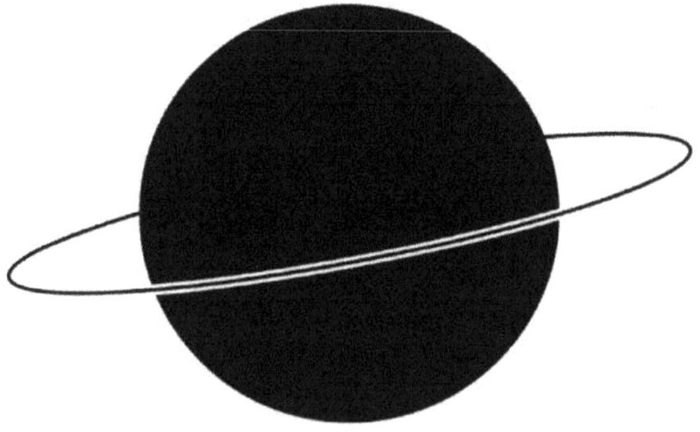

CHAPTER 21

Lights flashed on the navigation panel. Sev handled each alarm, aware that the old skiff was misjudging the sudden altitude change as a cause for concern. But the descent was natural. Ahead, the blue thread of atmosphere stretched across the view pane. Terra Firma lay ahead, as green and ominous as ever.

Sev buckled herself in. She missed her father like this, when making course adjustments and manning the navigation at the same time proved almost too much to handle. But if her father had been here and could fly, then she wouldn't need to go to Terra Firma.

She blew out a breath, one hand on the guidance system and the other one on the nav. The stars swung left in the view pane as the ship canted with the course correction. There was a rumbling, the ear-splitting crackle of heat. Ahead, the green orb grew large and unavoidable, rushing toward her at an incredible speed. She was going to Terra Firma now; there was no turning back.

The stars disappeared, replaced by the blue-green sky of Terra Firma. With a touch of the controls, the ship righted itself; the thrusters died. The force of it threw her back against the seat. She looked outside, and the air was hazy with spores, even this high up. Her hands vibrated on the controls. Trees rushed past as the ship descended, breaking limbs as it went. She struggled to lean forward, to manage the nav. The ground was close, growing larger by the second. With a shaky hand, Sev hit the flaps and let gravity do the rest.

After a terrifying few seconds of turbulence, the skiff landed on Terra Firma.

Sev took a few moments to orient herself, listening to the cooling engines tick and decompress. She'd really done it, she thought to herself. She was here.

Sev unbuckled and slid out of the navigator's seat. The ship sat askew on the surface; the landing had been a bad one. She could barely stand upright.

Takeoff would be tricky in this position. The skiff usually lifted off exactly upright from a flat surface. Angled liftoffs could quickly throw you off course, or worse, send you spinning into oblivion.

She'd worry about that when the time came. For now, she had work to do.

Sev approached her suit. She'd laid it out flat in the Black, but the rocky landing had slid it against the far wall of the ship. She held it up, unzipping and unbuckling the fasteners, and stepped into it.

Being in a suit again felt surreal, and not in the familiar, nostalgic way that happy memories did. It felt claustrophobic. Putting it on brought back all those moments she spent in a suit close to dying—spore sick in the miner's tent, shouldering Phoenix's weakened body after the harvester's attack, cutting herself on the second trip, the paralyzing fear.

She blinked and took a few slow, deep breaths. Phoenix had taught her deep breathing to combat the aftermath of nightmares so many years ago, when she would awake soaked in sweat and hyperventilating, when all she could see when she shut her eyes was Phoenix injured or dead, or some unnamed threat coming out of the wilds of Terra Firma to end her once and for all. Sev had either dreamed of Terra Firma or traveled there too many times for natural peace. For many years, inner peace was something she had to work at, something she had to seek.

After a few breaths, she felt better. Her heart rate slowed. She tucked herself into the suit, checking the filter before securing the helmet. It shone fully charged—a bit of luck.

Sev gathered up her pack, making sure everything was secure. She had brought enough nutrition for a day and a night on Terra Firma, barring anything unforeseen. It had been years since she'd stepped foot on the planet, and her memory of the topography was sketchy.

The green marshes held the highest concentration of spores…she remembered that. If she could find them, she could get what she needed and get out.

She secured the ship, putting everything in standby mode in case she needed to make a quick getaway. Almost as an afterthought, she picked up the air gun, securing it to her hip.

She was finally ready. She took a deep breath, holding it for a few seconds before blowing it out. Her hand shook on the hatch, as if her body was resisting leaving the ship. She fought her instincts and turned the lever.

The hatch hissed open. Her suit remained sealed, but sensors inside her helmet told her the air outside was humid and thick. She breathed in the dry, spore-free air flowing from her filter and tried to wrap herself in some semblance of safety.

But no one had ever been safe on Terra Firma, least of all her.

Sev stepped through the hatch. The planet's sun filtered through the haze, creating a verdant film over everything.

She was not where she expected. At least, it didn't look like she was.

Panic tightened her chest. Had she miscalculated the landing point? The coordinates she'd set had taken her to the clearing beside the calcet pit. But there was no more clearing. Plants towered over her; trees reached so high she couldn't see the top of them. She couldn't see her feet, as buried in the underbrush as they were. Her heart was thrumming in her ears. This was not right, she thought. Not right at all. She turned around, looking back at the ship.

Wilderness surrounded it. Leafy trees and vines pressed in on all sides. She looked up; the trail the skiff had cut through the trees was obvious, a scorched line of broken branches and singed greenery.

She listened intently. The high-pitched trill of insects rang in the air, loud in an otherwise quiet, still world.

Terra Firma had changed. It was not the planet she remembered, and that scared her more than she wanted to admit.

She looked toward the Pit, only it wasn't there. Overgrowth had swallowed it with wild vines, the stalks of plants. Her mouth grew dry. Vaguely, she wondered how she would ever find calcet now, and if Uncle Dak could ever forgive her for breaking their bargain.

Sev pulled out her handheld nav. The green marshes were west; maybe if she walked in that direction long enough, she'd find her way.

She shouldered her pack where it had slipped down on her arm and headed out opposite the murky sun and into the wild unknown of Terra Firma.

CHAPTER 22

By her chrono, it had been hours. She was exhausted, her limbs heavy with fatigue and exertion, her arms shaky with the effort it took to cut through the heavy vines and plants, to forge a trail. She held a large blade and swung it in front of her, clearing a path. Her muscles ached.

Sev remembered when this terrain was all trails. There'd always been plant life on Terra Firma, but it had never grown so wildly. The intermittent human element on Terra Firma kept the brush beat back. The danger here kept their greed in check.

She frowned. She never could fathom the greed element…why calcet drove some people wild. But hard living made you hungry, and that she understood.

The sun was slipping below the canopy, casting the world into green twilight. It would be dark soon, she thought, regardless of the time of day. Life below the canopy of Terra Firma was never bright.

It was too late to turn back, and the green marshes were nowhere in sight. So, she'd have to camp.

The idea of any kind of rest sparked in her brain, making her thirst for it. She felt rung out, drenched with sweat inside her suit and aching for a respite.

Sev hacked the underbrush until she'd cleared a small campsite. They'd be no fire tonight, as humid as it was on Terra Firma, and while her suit was not climate controlled, it was thick. She should be ok.

She regretted leaving the thermal insulator she'd packed for space travel; it was safely on the ship, and sadly, of no use to her when she needed it.

The night grew colder. Her senses seemed amplified—the mysterious noises she'd heard before became louder, more urgent. She tried to ignore them, and darkness descended like a shroud. Sev retrieved her glow lamp from her bag and turned it on. Its light cast unfamiliar shadows in the forest, causing her to stare wide-eyed and breathless into the brush.

She was alone on an alien planet. The realization weighed heavily on her, and despite her nervous nausea, her stomach rumbled. She reached for a nutrition pack, hooked it to her filter, and let it vacuum the contents into a tube inside her helmet. She sucked the viscous fluid, swallowing it down. It was lukewarm and unappetizing, but it would keep her going.

She curled on her side, hovering around the glow lamp like she would a fire. Sev covered her ears, trying to drown out the deafening sound of the night creatures that were there, but remained hidden, probably intrigued by the light.

She couldn't shake the feeling that she was being watched.

Her eyes flew open, ever vigilant. It had persisted ever since she'd stepped onto Terra Firma, the powerful sensation that she wasn't truly alone…that an unknown observer loomed just beyond her sight. The feeling left her unsettled, if not a little threatened. She was vulnerable and out of her element; if someone or something wanted to harm her, she was easy prey.

She lay like that for several moments, eyes wide and searching the dark. There was nothing but shadows beyond the tree line…infinite and black.

Sev had resolved to forget it, to brush it off as an overactive imagination and try to get some sleep, when the unmistakable sound of a stick snapping underfoot brought her back to wakefulness. Her body became rigid with fear. Her heart beat so rapidly she thought it might burst from her chest. Sev jolted upright, pulling the air gun from its holster and holding it out in front of her.

"Who's there?!" she called out, hoping to prompt the unseen assailant to reveal themselves. If she could see them, she could fight them, she reasoned. As long as they stayed hidden, they were at an advantage.

Nothing happened. No large, lumbering creature tearing through the bush to eat her alive. No exotic animal. Her hand shook where it held the air gun, but she did not lower it.

You're violent.

Sev blinked at the voice that bloomed on her consciousness. It was not hers, but she also didn't hear it. It was a thought, subtle but clear.

"Who said that?" she asked a little timidly, half afraid to learn the answer. Her gaze skittered over the landscape, or what she could see of it in the heavy darkness.

The shadows shifted and moved, but no one appeared.

I did, came the same gentle voice. The two words rang in her head as if someone had said them aloud, but they hadn't.

Sev scowled. "Show yourself," she threatened. "Show yourself, or I'll start shooting. It may be dark, but I'm bound to hit something, eventually."

The shadows shifted again, and Sev fired the weapon at the movement, as good as her word. Skittering footsteps rang out in retreat.

Sev stood there for a few seconds, unmoving. She knew she was being observed; she could feel the oil-slick slide of eyes over her skin.

Lower your weapon, came the serene voice. *Why are you so afraid?*

Sev frowned. "Because you're not supposed to be here," she said to no one. She turned, looking around. She saw nothing. If it had wanted to hurt her, it would've done so already, she reasoned. It would've attacked her in her sleep, when she was most defenseless. With a moment's trepidation, she holstered the weapon. The shadows moved, coalesced, and formed into a bipedal creature with skin the color of the forest.

The creature stepped out toward the light, where the reflection of the glow lamp danced on its shimmering camouflage skin. It had long thin arms, thin lips and enormous eyes. She shivered, astounded by what she was seeing.

"Drek's sake," Sev whispered.

The creature looked at her, its head canted curiously. *Who is Drek?*

Sev's mouth quirked. Her father was better suited for that question; his faith was stronger than hers. She put her hands on her hips. "A better question: Who are you?"

The creature moved forward a step, and Sev backed away. *We are the Verdani. We are the keepers of this land.*

Its thin lips never moved, but Sev heard every word in her mind. She stiffened a bit. If the Verdani saw her as a threat, she could be in real trouble.

She didn't know where this race of beings had come from…she'd never encountered their kind before on her trips to Terra Firma. Perhaps they had hidden; maybe they didn't even exist. She raised her hands, now weaponless.

"I mean you no harm," she said. "I'm here for my father. He became sick here many years ago…the spores are in his blood." She looked down, gathering herself. "If I don't bring back spores, he'll die."

Then, from the shadows, various shapes formed…more beings, all with the chameleon-like skin and large, unblinking eyes. Sev stood looking around the campsite. They surrounded her.

One Verdani stepped forth, its spindly arms out to the side. *Your father? He is one with the spores?*

A hushed tittering crowded her brain, many voices converging at once. The Verdani that first spoke to her motioned with a thin hand, and the others quieted.

The spores are sacred. You cannot take them from our planet, he told her.

Sev deflated. The imminent loss hit her like a brick. If she couldn't take the spores, her father would never make it. He might even die before she got to say goodbye, something Sev couldn't fathom.

We can give them to you. For your father, the being said. *If he is one with the spores, then he is "a gata." In our language, it means holy.*

She made a little sound of shock; relieved tears stung her eyes, and with no way to wipe them away, they blurred her vision before spilling down her cheeks.

"Thank you so much," Sev muttered. "My father is a good man. He deserves your kindness."

The being made an audible noise, a trilling sound not unlike what she'd heard before, as darkness had crept over the planet. *So do you. We have seen your heart, young traveler. It lies with your family.*

Sev said nothing. The being motioned with its hand, and the others dissolved into shadow, lost in the tapestry of the thick forest.

Rest tonight. We will go tomorrow, when it is light.

She sat back down around the glow lamp. The shadows didn't seem as frightening as they did before, nor did she feel so alone.

CHAPTER 23

S ev awoke the next morning, and the forest of Terra Firma was alive with the chirps and whirs of insects and the melodious trills of the distant Verdani.

She thought of Phoenix, first thing. How it'd been so long since he'd felt the sun on his face…how his skin had gone sallow from sickness and artificial light.

Phoenix would not agree with what she was doing. He was self-sacrificing. He would hate that she was putting herself in harm's way, especially for him.

But as much as she loved her father, she knew he wasn't always right.

Sev was confident she could do this, or she would've never come here. She would've spent her father's last days by his bedside. She wouldn't have wasted time and risked her life on a foolhardy mission just to prove a point.

Sev opened her pack and pulled out some nutrition. She hooked it to her filter and waited for the contents to make its way into the tube inside her helmet. She looked up, and there was a familiar rustling in the trees. A Verdani stepped out of the brush, its skin dappled with splotches of green to match its surroundings.

It's time to go. We must hurry if we are to make the caves before dark. The journey is long.

She finished her nutrition and packed her gear away. Sev could see the Verdani clearly now in the light of day, their curious, shifting skin, their large, mirrored eyes.

"Why are we going to a cave? I thought the green marshes would have the most spores?"

The Verdani hummed. *The green marshes are dangerous, even to us. Our caves are safer. Come, you will see.*

Sev followed. The Verdani was alone, though Sev suspected there were others just out of view. They seemed to travel together. She followed it silently through the brush, taking time to observe how Terra Firma had changed.

Terra Firma now was not the planet of her youth. It was still deadly, still dangerous, but now it was a wild and untamed place. Greed had ravaged this planet for decades, beckoning harvesters with its precious gems. She'd seen it herself, what people would do for calcet.

All of that was over. The scars had healed, now. Terra Firma had reclaimed its land.

Up ahead, the forest opened to a clearing. This part of Terra Firma was unfamiliar to her, and not because of the overgrowth. There were runes carved into the trees, and the sun beamed down from an opening in the canopy, spores thick in the single shaft of light. Small structures stood amidst the undergrowth. Inside the darkened dwellings, she could see the reflections of the mirrored eyes of the Verdani.

"Is this where you live?"

The Verdani made a calm trilling sound. *This is our home*, the Verdani replied.

Sev looked beyond the structure. Small camouflaged beings moved in the distance, dipping in and out of the tree line. It looked almost playful.

"Are those children?" Sev asked. It surprised her, though it shouldn't have.

Of course. Family bonds are important to the Verdani. That is why the story of your father moved us to help you. Also, he is a gata, or so I was told.

Sev nodded, though she walked behind the Verdani and out of view. Her guide hiked the rough terrain vigorously, and she had to hustle to keep up. They passed the clearing, and Sev looked back once more to see the little village and the way they lived. Mirrored eyes looked back at her, curious, but not unfriendly.

How did your father become a gata?

Sev considered, stepping over a fallen log. "He had an injury here, years ago. He inhaled the spores, and they infected his wounds. It is deadly for humans to breathe the air on Terra Firma. That's why I wear this suit."

What happened?

She frowned. She did not want to recount the history between her and Del, of how Phoenix's filter became ruined or that Del shot him. It was still painful, still complicated after all these years.

She cleared her throat. "His, uh, his filter became damaged. Mine did too, for that matter. We were both using mine, and it just gave out."

The Verdani hummed. *Yet, he did not die. Nor did you. Your fragile human bodies survived, somehow.*

Sev couldn't suppress a smile. "I guess so," she said. "I never really thought about it."

The being made a sharp series of trills, then grew quiet. *Then you are a gata, too.*

She said nothing. She did not want to think of what that meant for her and her father, that this alien race had found some kinship with them, but if it helped her carry out her mission here, she didn't mind it.

Those who breathe the spores become one with the land, the Verdani said. *They are a gata. We are a gata.*

The Verdani stopped and turned to her. "I can speak to you now, like I do with the Verdani."

Sev's mouth fell open in shock. "You can talk."

The Verdani nodded. "The caves are just up ahead."

Its voice was light and lilting. Not what Sev expected at all. She hitched up her pack and pushed her exhausted legs one more mile until they stood at the mouth of a great cave wreathed in green and brown vines, the twining limbs of nearby trees. Had the Verdani not pointed it out, Sev might've never found it.

The Verdani stepped back to blend with a nearby tree. Sev watched as their skin changed from green to blotchy brown to match the tree trunk. "I will wait for you here. I cannot enter."

Sev nodded. She stepped toward the cave, reaching up and moving some vines away from the entrance. It was so dark within that she could barely see a few feet in front of her. She could hear the wind howling from the depths, felt the breeze as resistance against her suit.

With a deep breath, Sev stepped inside.

The darkness swallowed her at once, momentarily disorienting her. How could she go on, she wondered, if she couldn't see? Then she remembered Uncle Dak's headlamp.

Sev put down her pack and unzipped it. She fumbled around until she felt the solid square shape, the elastic headband. She tied it around her wrist, unable to wear it properly with her helmet in place.

Light flooded the cave. The walls, the ceiling, every visible surface sparkled with iridescent light. There were shallow pools of water on the floor of the cave. A rainbow sheen shimmered on their surfaces, catching in the light from the headlamp.

She pushed farther into the cave, careful where she stepped, but still occasionally stumbling over a sparkling stalagmite. The needle on her handheld nav spun wildly; there was a gravitational pull here that was not on the surface, and Sev wondered briefly what that may mean.

The air grew cold; she could feel it through her suit. Tiny creatures, little more than balls of fur, scurried out of sight of her light and into cracks in the walls of the cave. It made her smile to see another form of life other than the Verdani.

There was much about Terra Firma that she didn't know, and it continued to amaze her. She'd never considered that it might support life outside its dangerous plants and toxic air. But Terra Firma had revealed itself to be a complex and intriguing place.

But still deadly, she reminded herself. Given her history here, that was not something she was likely to forget.

Up ahead, Sev heard rushing water. The light from the entrance behind her was so far away she could no longer see it. She was deep within the cave. Silently, she willed the little headlamp to keep shining, lest she become lost within.

After a time, she arrived at the sound. There was a beautiful waterfall emptying into a deep, crystalline pool. She stood there for a few seconds, dazzled by the sight.

On the surface of the pool, glowing iridescent and thick, were the spores.

Her breath caught in her throat. They were so thick here they'd coalesced into a floating colony undulating on the surface of the water. She tapped her filter, checking its charge. It was half-full. She would have to hurry.

She withdrew the vials, the little spatula. She thought of the enormity of this gift, of what the Verdani was allowing her to do. These spores were sacred to them, and she was taking some of them with her. She felt enormous gratitude.

Sev held the vial to the surface and scraped the spores into the tube. She filled both, unsure of how much she needed and erring on the side of caution.

Sev capped the tubes securely, holding them up to the light. *I'm coming, Daddy,* she thought as she looked at their slight glow, the sinister way they bubbled. She slipped them into her pack. Sev dipped her hands in the water, making sure no spores clung to her gloves. As she was staring into the depths, she saw something shining at the bottom.

She reached further in, her curiosity winning out. Her hand closed around what felt like a stone, and she pulled it up.

She gasped. It was a piece of calcet, the pure gem and not the membrane. It was not the peachy hue she was familiar with; this calcet was as blue as the Dobani Sea. Something rare and wondrous. While not two pieces, Uncle Dak would get his payment, after all.

Sev secured it in her pack, eager to leave. She took a moment and looked around the dreamlike cave, committing it to memory. She could see why the Verdani might consider this place sacred.

Sev started the long journey back, her heart full.

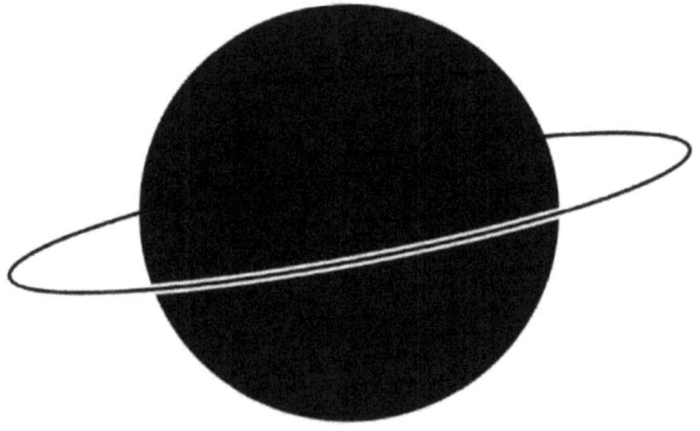

CHAPTER 24

The light from the cave's entrance was up ahead, growing larger by the step. Her filter beeped, and she checked the readout.

One quarter full. She'd exerted herself in the cave, and now her filter was almost empty.

Time was of the essence now. She had to get back to the ship.

The Verdani was waiting for her, as true as their word. The sun had shifted; she must've been below ground for several hours, maybe more.

"Thank you," she breathed. And the Verdani nodded. It turned to lead her away from the cave, but she stopped it.

She remembered the calcet, the piece she'd taken from the cave. It didn't feel right for her to keep it without their knowledge. Now that she knew the Verdani, she respected their customs.

"I found something," she began. "I need it, but I wanted to ask first. If it's ok."

She withdrew the calcet from her pack and held it out; the ambient light from the canopy caught on its rare blue color, and it shone with a curious fire.

The Verdani said nothing. It canted its head slightly, looking at Sev with intrigue.

"You did not ask before, when you were with the others."

It shamed her. She was a part of Terra Firma's long history of greed as much as anyone. The calcet rush. The killing. She and Phoenix had even come back to make their fortune.

"I know," she confessed. "But I understand now. I wouldn't have taken it if I hadn't promised it to someone. For helping me."

The Verdani hummed. It stretched out its hand and covered hers with its long fingers. Its skin was cool to the touch. "It is yours."

Her filter beeped again, and the Verdani looked down at it where it hung attached to the front of her suit.

"We must hurry. It is nearing your time."

They hiked for an hour, passing by unfamiliar, large structures that must've been ancient ruins.

They neared a clearing that felt familiar, that conjured ghosts from her past to spring to the forefront of her mind. Sev stopped to catch her breath; she could feel the struggling filter…the effort it took to churn out fresh air to keep her going.

"Wait," she called out, and the Verdani stopped. "I know this place."

Sev looked around. She stood in the middle of the clearing, trying to orient herself. Suddenly, she was twelve years old again. The ozone of a discharged air gun hung in the air…a scuffle. When the dust settled, two men lay on the ground.

Sev shook her head. She was back in the present, again. The same clearing, but a different time. She looked near the tree line, and there was a bright flag of orange. The sleeve of a suit.

Del's remains rested in the undergrowth, half buried beside a tree.

She swallowed, emotions rising in her throat. Suddenly everything felt too real, in hyper-focus. She could feel the thick vegetation at her feet, clinging to her suit, could almost taste the oppressive air. She looked, and the Verdani was waiting for her, looking on impassively.

Sev walked over to where the brush had covered it…the gentle mound. His suit, bright orange like hers had been that day, shined through the undergrowth, undulled by time and the elements. She reached and cleared some of the brush away, exposing his body to the light.

His helmet was clouded by time, and she wiped it clean with her hand. Beneath, Del's skull lay inside, bleached white by spores, the flesh eaten away.

She closed her eyes against the tears…memories of her birth father, moments she had not thought of in years, came rushing back, dizzying her with their ferocity. She went to her knees, overcome with emotion.

With her eyes shut, those moments became even clearer. She and Del sharing a ration bar under a lean-to in Central City. Del trading for an extra nutrition pack. He always let her eat first.

She opened her eyes. Del had pushed her first into that calcet pit all those years ago, she remembered. She'd gone obediently…because she had wanted to help. Because he was her father and he had told her to.

She stood on shaky legs and looked down at where he lay. He was not all bad, but he wasn't all good. He had loved her in his own way. Not like Phoenix loved her, selflessly and without condition, but as much as his single-minded avarice and self-preservation allowed him to.

She silently thanked him for her life, for caring for her as best he could. Tears were running freely now, with no way to wipe them away. It surprised her. She thought she had made peace with Del a long time ago, but seeing his bones had resurrected an old pain.

Her filter beeped, insistent and loud. There was no time to bury him. She could only say goodbye.

She sniffed and straightened herself. Off to the side, the Verdani looked on curiously.

"I'm ok," she began, staring down at the partially buried corpse on the floor of the forest. "A good man raised me. I'm happy."

Del's pale skull shone in the low light, empty eye sockets staring blindly. The sun was setting. But the ship wasn't far.

"Goodbye, Dad," Sev said, her emotions in check now. She felt liberated by the words, as if a heavy weight had just lifted from her chest. She felt free.

She turned and followed the Verdani out of the clearing. The Verdani did not ask, and she was glad. She had left Del where he fell, and the land could claim him.

♦ ♦ ♦

The ship came into view sometime later; it really was in a precarious position for takeoff, tilted as it was, but it was what she had, so she would make it work.

The sight of the ship gave her renewed energy. She quickened her pace until she stood in its shadow as the canopy darkened into night.

Suddenly, the Verdani were all around her, their reflective eyes catching the dying light. She looked at each of them soberly and held up her hand in farewell.

"I will never speak of you," she assured them solemnly. "And I will never return."

One of the Verdani stepped forward. "This is the way of our people."

Sev's lip quivered, and she bit back the emotion in her voice. "I will never forget your kindness and your generosity for what you have given me and my father. He will live now because of you. And a part of you in him."

The Verdani nodded. "A gata," they muttered. "May his years be long."

Sev smiled. She turned without another word and climbed the ramp to the hatch. She stood in the opening, looking out over Terra Firma and its inhabitants for the last time. This visit had changed her…enriched her. She was a better person because of it.

The ship's hatch sealed with a hiss, and she sighed in relief.

She stripped her suit and sat at the nav. Sev punched in the coordinates for Ocarro and fired the engines.

She let the ship sit for a few moments, thrusters warming. The diagonal liftoff would throw her off course, and she barely had enough fuel for the trip back.

It didn't matter. The course correction had to be done. She pulled the lever, and the ship shook. Limbs and vines fell away as the skiff carved a new trail through the thick canopy of Terra Firma.

CHAPTER 25

Pearla sat within the circle, holding a cup of tea. "It's an old Ocarri recipe," a member had told her. "It will give the baby lots of hair."

She was still getting used to the fact that she would soon be a mother.

"That's all for today," Prescott said in closing. "Remember, take care of yourselves. There's only one of you."

He smiled and left the group. Probably to take care of patients, she thought. Prescott was good at leading the group…he had a kind and understanding spirit that reminded her of Phoenix.

Pearla sipped the tea; it was slightly bitter with a sweet aftertaste. She looked up and saw Fallon walking toward her.

"I'm so glad you've joined us," the woman beamed. She was an off-worlder too, tall and willowy, with a graceful neck and long auburn hair. She had bright green eyes that reminded her of Sev.

Pearla had not heard from her in so long and felt her absence acutely.

Anything could've happened to her by now, Pearla thought gravely. From what she'd heard of Sev and Phoenix's stories, Terra Firma was a dangerous place fraught with deadly plants and poisonous air. She looked down, tightening her fingers around the cup, and sent up a silent prayer for her safety.

"Hey hon, where did you just go now?"

Fallon touched her arm gently, just enough to get her attention. Pearla smiled softly and took a sip of her tea. "I was just thinking," she said.

Fallon furrowed her brow. "About Phoenix?"

Pearla walked them over to a pair of chairs and they sat down. "About Sev."

The woman made a piteous face. "She still missing, huh?"

Pearla did not answer. She'd told no one about Sev going to Terra Firma, or the situation with Phoenix needing spores. Pearla till didn't know who she could trust on this alien planet, as nice as some people might be.

She shook her head. "Still gone," she said sadly. "And I worry about her. She's a capable girl, but she's young. I thought I could save the world too when I was sixteen."

Fallon laughed. "Didn't we all!" She leaned over her own hot beverage, almost conspiratorially. "So, how are you feeling, Pearla?" she asked in a hushed voice. "Any movement?"

She glanced down at Pearla's still-flat belly as if to emphasize her meaning, but there was no need. Ever since Fallon had found out Pearla was pregnant, she'd been very interested in her well-being.

"No," Pearla answered truthfully. "None. Part of me still doesn't believe it."

Fallon smiled. "Well, believe it. Maris is rarely wrong. She may be a little kookie, but her instincts are spot on."

Pearla smiled. She was keeping her meeting with Prescott and the scan that proved she was pregnant to herself, for now.

"How is your husband?" Pearla asked her, hoping to steer the conversation away from herself.

Fallon blew across the top of her beverage. It smelled like stim. "He's better," she said, brightening. "Prescott says the Lumiers are working." She sighed, looking into the distance. "I'll be so happy when we can just get back to normal. If I can just have him back the way he was, I'll never nag him about picking up his clothes ever again."

Pearla huffed, endeared by Fallon's musings. "Phoenix is very tidy. And helpful. I never have that problem."

Fallon rolled her eyes. "You're lucky, hon. Your life sounds so perfect."

She felt the tears sting her eyes before she realized she was crying. "I miss him," Pearla said. "He's right there in that bed, but I miss the way he made me laugh. His giving nature. The way he loves both me and Sev." She looked up at Fallon, stricken. "When does it get better?"

Fallon smiled sadly. "Only when they do," she told her. "Right now, it's just rough. But hey, you've got the baby! And you've got me. You're not truly alone."

Pearla looked down, afraid of the confession poised on her lips. "I-I don't think I can do it," she whispered.

Fallon reached out, placing a hand on her shoulder. "Do what, dear? Women have been having babies since the beginning of the age."

She shook her head. "No, Fallon. I don't think I can handle it by myself. The doctors said the Lumiers will take a year, maybe longer. The baby will be here by then. And I'll be alone."

Fallon set down her tea and leaned over, putting her arm around her. "Oh honey. You're not alone. You won't be alone. Phoenix will wake up, and you can tell him your good news. It will give him even more of a reason to fight for you."

Her lips quivered. "I'm not even sure if he wants a baby," Pearla whispered, hushed and timid. "We never talked about it."

Fallon smiled. "As much as he seems to love you? He'll love this baby too. Just you wait and see."

She raised her head, a hopeful smile on her face. "You think so?"

The woman grinned. "I'm positive."

It satisfied Pearla. She wiped her eyes and finished her tea. They sat in companionable silence for a few moments until Pearla stood and tossed the cup in the trash. "I better get back. I've been gone awhile."

Fallon considered. "It's been good for you, getting out. Even if you're still in the hospital, just getting out of that room is a good thing."

"Yeah," Pearla breathed. She gave her a little wave. "Thanks for the talk. See you around, Fallon."

The woman smiled. "I'll be by later to check in. Go enjoy your time with Phoenix."

Pearla left her and walked for a while down the overly bright Medical Center hall. The meeting room wasn't too far from Phoenix, but it was far enough to feel like she'd got out for a bit. It felt good. It felt like she was doing something other than sitting and feeling sorry for herself.

Up ahead, there was noise and activity. Alarms were going off by someone's door, and a team of doctors rushed that way, their coats flying behind them. It was very close to where Phoenix was.

Dread filled her stomach like a lead weight. She unconsciously walked faster until she was sprinting down the hall toward Phoenix's room.

She rounded the corner. Pearla could see inside Phoenix's room through the large observation windows. A red light was flashing over his bed.

Doctors and medics surrounded him. A few of them held injections, bags of fluids. Another doctor did chest compressions, trying to revive him.

Oh, Drek, she thought miserably. *I cannot lose him now. Not with this baby coming. Not with Sev gone.*

She burst into the room, nearly out of breath. "What's happening?" she panted. "What's going on?"

A medic clasped her arm, urging her outside. "You can't be in here," he snapped. "We're trying to save this man's life."

Behind him, the doctor was still doing chest compressions. Monitors beeped. The red light was still flashing.

She jerked free of his hold, looking at him with a hard gaze. "I'm all he has!" she spat. "I'm not going anywhere."

Prescott heard her and broke away from the team of doctors. He dismissed the medic who'd tried to shoo her out and led her to a corner of the room. "Pearla, Phoenix is having a reaction to the Lumiers. His body is rejecting it. If we can't give him medications to stabilize him, he'll die."

She doubled over, grief taking her breath. "Pearla," Prescott urged her. "I can't make you leave, but it's going to be hard on you if you stay here. I'm not sure you want to see him like this."

She shook her head, an adamant refusal. "I won't leave him," she asserted. "I want to be here."

He patted her arm. "I must get back. Stay right here. We're going to do what we can for him."

Pearla watched from the corner, careful not to get in the way. The man doing compressions had stopped; she wasn't sure what that meant.

A doctor was injecting him with something. There was a mask on his face, and so many medics around that she couldn't see him. One of them backed away, then another. The red light went out. The machines quieted to a low hum, an intermittent beep.

"What does that mean?" she all but yelled from the corner. "Will someone talk to me?!"

Prescott approached her. "He's stable. For now. The next few hours will tell the tale. You should try to get some rest, Pearla. You'll be no good to him, exhausted as you are."

She shook her head. "No, I won't leave him. I'll be right here until he wakes up."

Prescott said nothing. He turned and left with the other doctors, leaving her alone.

She looked at Phoenix. There were tubes and wires either coming out of him or going into him nearly everywhere she looked. His chest…his arm. A heavy mask covered his handsome face, the hose vibrating with every mechanical breath. He was pale, ashen, not his usual healthy color.

She pulled up the familiar chair as close as she could by the bed. She found his hand where it rested atop the cover; it was cold, his skin papery.

"Phoenix? You've got to wake up soon, hon. We've got to have a long talk." She squeezed his hand, reinforcing the point. "I've got something I want to tell you, but I want you to hear it…truly hear it and respond. Ok?"

She looked at his closed eyes, the mask over his face, and frowned. Tears welled in her eyes. "Oh, Phoenix. Please come back to me! I need you, love. I'm all alone now. Sev is gone, and I've got no way of contacting her. My heart is so burdened. Please."

She placed a hand over her belly, trying to feel the tiny life within. It was still very unreal to her…very much beyond what she had ever imagined for herself. But this baby was a part of her and Phoenix. It would know immense love.

Pearla wondered briefly how she would tell Sev. For so long, she was Phoenix's only child. Would she feel threatened by this new baby? Isolated? Forgotten?

No, Pearla thought. She knew Sev's heart. Sev would love this baby too; she would be the best big sister any child could ever ask for.

Pearla crossed her arms over the bed and laid her head down on them. Her eyes were closing of their own volition; her body was exhausted. She fought to stay awake, but the stress of the last few hours hit her hard. She listened to the drone and hum of the machines, the mask breathing life into Phoenix, until her eyes slipped closed in sleep.

CHAPTER 26

The sun was deceptively warm through the glass ceiling of the greenhouse, hitting his bare arms where he'd rolled up the sleeves of his jumpsuit and the back of his neck. Greenhouses were common on Ocarro, where snow was prevalent all solar year, and the ground stayed frozen even through the "warm" months.

He dug his spade into the warm, moist earth. The controls kept the climate temperate; precipitation fell from sprinklers installed overhead. For a moment, if Soren forgot all the other prisoners and the shackles around his ankles, he could imagine he was in his own little garden at home.

It was for this reason that he didn't mind this work detail. It got him out of his cell and gave him something to do. Allowed him to work up a sweat. If he couldn't save lives, he'd rather be cultivating plants, anyway.

His mother liked plants. He could remember her before she'd become sick, her tending the plants in their small greenhouse, wearing a hat to protect her fair skin from the sun. Soren had been right in step with her, helping her carry the produce she harvested in a basket that was almost too big for him. The thought of her brought a smile to his face.

He hadn't realized he'd stopped working, standing there leaning on his spade. One prisoner pushed him, shaking him from his revelry. "You going to stand there all day? You work or you'll get us all in trouble."

The prisoner was gruff and much larger than Soren. Soren muttered an apology, sinking his spade into the earth and weeding around a stalk of vegetables.

Cyrus, who was working beside him, overheard.

"Watch how you talk to my friend, or I'll gut ya."

The other prisoner scoffed. "It will be a warm day on Ocarro before I'm scared of a one-eyed old man like you," he shot back.

Cyrus stared him down, enraged. Soren stood caught in the middle. He turned to the older man, his hands up. "Hey, maybe let it go," Soren pled with Cyrus, but it was no use. The prisoner had injured his pride.

"Yeah? Maybe come over and see for yourself," Cyrus taunted. He held his spade out in a threatening gesture. "I've got one good fight left in me yet!"

The prisoner punched him without warning, and Cyrus reeled, stumbling back. He fell between the rows, blood gushing from his nose.

Soren turned to the prisoner. There was anger in his beady eyes, the black depths dark and glittering with unspent rage. "You want some too, eh?"

Soren balled up his fists. He did, truth be told. It was frustrating being locked in here with worse men than him. Men who had hurt people…men who had killed. Soren felt caged. He felt suffocated. The ire rose within him.

The man took advantage of his distraction and struck him first, knocking him back into another prisoner. They pushed him off, and he ducked another blow as he was steadying himself.

Soren swung wildly, aiming for the man's eye. His fist snagged on his nose instead, and he felt the cartilage crunch beneath his fists. His knuckles cracked; some felt broken.

The man looked startled. His hands flew up to cover his mangled nose. Blood gushed from beneath his fingers as he tried to staunch the flow, and he whimpered. The man swung again, missed, and Soren hit him square in the jaw.

It was the last punch thrown. Guards pulled Soren off him; Soren was rigid with rage, his hand gone numb from pain. "Take him to the Infirmary," another guard said. Soren looked back, his feet dragging along the rows of plants to see Cyrus dotting his nose with his sleeve. He had a big smile on his face.

Soren shook his head. He wished he could take it back, to not get involved, but it was unavoidable, in retrospect. The prisoner had hit a mouthy old man, a defenseless, sick old man, basically harmless, and then he'd turned on him. He had to defend himself.

Unfortunately, it would look like he was the aggressor. The guards only saw him hit the man in the jaw, and not what had come before. He was well and truly cooked. He'd probably never see the gardens again, or the outside of his cell, for that matter.

The guards led him to the Infirmary, hustling him inside. It was a surprisingly well-appointed medical facility. There were cabinets of supplies, medical-grade machinery, and several empty beds. There appeared to be no patients now, and he was glad.

The lead doctor met them at the door. He was older than Soren, but not what he would consider elderly. Middle-aged might be more appropriate. He had the natural dark hair and dark eyes typical of the Ocarri, but his skin was a shade darker than most. "Well, what do we have here, fellows?" he asked, his eyes alight with humor. He had the air of a doctor who had seen one too many prison fights, one too many silly skirmishes between violent people.

"Oh, this scum picked a fight with an old man and another prisoner. Broke his hand for the effort."

The other guard laughed. "Patch him up and call us, and we'll escort him back to his cell."

The doctor looked at Soren, concerned. He led him to the edge of one of the examination tables and patted the thin mattress. "Up you go," he told Soren, and Soren obliged, his left hand cradling the hurt one.

The guards left, and the doctor gingerly took Soren's hand and began testing the knuckles. Soren winced, trying to flex his fingers.

"Only two of them are broken," Soren said matter-of-factly.

The doctor huffed. "You a doctor now?" he quipped. "Guess there's no reason to scan you then, since you already know." The doctor held up the scanner anyway, ignoring his claim, and scanned his hand. Two beeps intoned, affirming Soren was right.

Soren frowned. "I'm not a doctor now," he said, his voice hushed. "I was though. First year medic. My name is Soren."

The doctor whistled. "How do you go from saving lives to harming people? Doesn't fit the code."

Soren pulled his hand away, frustrated. "I wasn't trying to hurt anyone. I didn't hit Cyrus. He's my friend. I hit the other guy, but it was in self-defense."

The doctor smiled, going to the cabinet for some plaster and wrappings. "It's always in self-defense," he said knowingly. "But you still don't look like the type." He stuck his hand out for Soren to shake it, but remembered his hurt dominant hand. "I'm Jol. I'm the head physician here. Well, the only physician."

Soren said nothing. He sat there sullenly as the doctor mixed the plaster and wrapped his hand. It would dry and harden, allowing the factures to heal. He wouldn't be able to use it for at least a week.

"You're right; I'm not the type," Soren muttered. He watched as the doctor worked. He had a gentle touch. The doctor reminded him of Prescott.

"What are you in for? White collar crime? Bank fraud, something like that?"

The doctor finished, gave him an injection, and put his supplies away. Soren appreciated the work. It was a neat job. "I helped someone escape a medical quarantine," he said.

The doctor narrowed his eyes, his brow furrowed. "And why would you do that?" he said. "Must've had a good reason."

Soren looked up at him, his mouth a firm line. "To save her father's life. He was my patient."

The doctor nodded, though Soren doubted he understood. There was so much more to the story than that. Truncating it to aiding a clumsy escape attempt seemed trite.

Jol considered him. "You like working in the gardens?"

Soren's mouth quirked upwards into a smile. "I did. Guess that's over now."

The doctor shrugged. "Come work for me. I get swamped on a full moon, or when the mess hall has a bad day. You see the best and worst of it in here, and I could use the help."

Soren's eyes widened. "You really mean it?"

He smiled. "Yes. Do what you were born to do. It will make you feel better about being here."

Soren lowered his head. "I doubt that," he said. "It's unclear what will happen to me now. Breaking medical code is a serious offense."

The doctor inclined his head. He said nothing at first, as if he were parsing his words. "It can be, yes. On Ocarro, certainly. But not every rule is in your patient's best interest. Something easy to forget."

It surprised Soren. He'd never heard another doctor speak that aloud…even suggesting breaking medical protocol was punishable by law. It's why he was here. The Medical Center had been lenient with him for a long time. Only when they caught him red-handed did they act.

"You really believe that?"

The doctor nodded. "With everything I am." He crossed his arms over his chest. "The system is flawed. I've seen it swallow good men." He looked back at him, his eyebrows up in question. "So, will you take the job or not?"

Soren smiled and held up his cast. "If you don't mind a one-handed doctor for a while."

The doctor pushed off the edge of the exam table, a wry grin on his face. "Better than no doctor at all. I'll talk to the Director. You can start in the morning."

He pressed a button on the wall, and within a few moments, the two guards from before appeared at the door. "This one is ready to go," the doctor instructed them.

The guards handled him a little roughly, and Soren drew his cast closer to his body, protecting his hand from further damage. They led him down the dimly lit hallway. He still had shackles on his feet.

"Someone called for you earlier," one of them said casually. "They set a date for your trial."

Soren perked up. "Oh yeah? When does the long arm of Ocarri law reach out and pat me on the back?"

The guard chuckled. "You get what's coming to you in two days, kid."

Soren swallowed, his stomach dropping out. Two days was not long at all. He didn't know if he could get in contact with Prescott by then. It was hard to get messages out.

They reached the cell door, the bars ominous and oppressive. Cyrus was in his usual spot, an ice pack on his nose. They unshackled him and pushed him inside.

He sat down on the edge of the dingy cot. His arm throbbed; the injection Jol had given him was already wearing off. He didn't mind the pain, though. It reminded him he was alive.

"You ok?" Cyrus asked him. He sounded tired.

Soren considered. He had a broken hand and an unknown fate hanging over his head. It couldn't get much worse.

"Yeah," he said instead, keeping his misery to himself. "I'm fine."

Cyrus harrumphed, seeing right through his lie. "Me too," he said through his swollen nose. "I'll keep my mouth shut next time. Maybe."

CHAPTER 27

Sev rested, content as she was with the ship's course and the fuel she had left after the correction. Her margin for error upon reentry was razor thin, now. She'd have to be careful. One touch of the thrusters too long and she would fly into Ocarro's already-volatile atmosphere uncontrolled.

She sipped a hydration pack and absently watched the controls. There was a tittering on one screen that caught her attention; she studied it for a moment, but it quickly disappeared. She brushed it off as interference. Then, there was an alarm bell.

She bolted upright, the hydration pack forgotten. A light on the console blinked, and there was a foreboding grinding noise that rang throughout the ship.

"Oh no," she said aloud. "Not this. Not now."

She tapped the screen. The interference was back, more insistent this time. A claxon rang out, a loud and obtrusive sound in the small space of the cockpit. The entire console was flashing red now. Things were spiraling out of control.

Sev quickly ran a diagnostic. She stood waiting for the assessment, her eyes wide, half afraid of what the readout might say.

The diagnostic machine spit out a long row of glyphs. Sev scanned the information, her hands tightening on the little slip of paper it produced.

There was a blocked ventilation duct, reducing the engine's ability to syphon oxygen. The blockage would have to be removed. Only it wasn't accessible from inside the cockpit. She'd have to go outside, into the Black.

Her stomach dropped out. She'd never spacewalked before. Ever. She had a rough idea of where the duct was…under the wing and not too far from the hatch, but it would be an incredibly risky endeavor.

If she didn't do it, the engine would eventually stall. The comm wasn't working; the years-long solar storm in this quadrant of space saw to that. She'd be dead in space, with no way to call for help. And it didn't take any stretch of the imagination to discern what would happen to Phoenix, then.

Sev took a breath, gathering her nerves. She had to do it. There was nothing for it.

She thought briefly about what her father would do. He wouldn't panic, that was for certain. He'd look at her and say, "let's get on with it, little mouse, before something else happens. Something worse."

It made her feel like she was doing the right thing, even if she doubted things could get any worse. Still, she thought as she was stepping into her suit, Phoenix would rise out of his bed and stop her himself if he knew she was going to perform a spacewalk with no backup.

She pulled the tether from the supplies closet. They'd never had to use it; Sev didn't even know how. She knew the basics…hook it to your suit and anchor it to something steady. What that would be, she wasn't sure.

She looked around; the crossbeam under the console would have to do. It would make sure she wouldn't float away, lost to the Black.

The thought sent a chill down her spine.

Sev strapped her tool pouch to her and made sure her helmet sealed. With a shaky breath, she opened the hatch into the infinite blackness of space.

The cold leached into her suit almost immediately, and she shivered. She didn't know if her suit was rated for space as most suits were; it was what Uncle Dak could find, and she was grateful. Still, she could feel the deep cold of space pressing in on her, stiffening her limbs and making it hard to move.

She stepped out onto the wing with a little nervous flutter in her belly. Her breathing was loud in her helmet, and the silence of the Black rang in her ears.

It reminded her of floating in the Dobani Sea…only the sea was warm and welcoming, not like space at all.

Another step, and she'd have to let go of the side of the ship. She'd be truly out in the Black for the first time.

Sev inched further out onto the wing and looked around, mesmerized. The stars were beautiful, unencumbered by the thick view pane of the cockpit. They were magnificent, and though she knew they were light years away, they looked as though she could reach out and put them in her pocket.

She stood for a few moments, her hand still on the hatch, gathering herself. *It's now or never,* she thought. With a shaky breath, she released the side of the hatch and dropped onto the wing.

The thrill that went through her at the release almost took her breath. She dug her gloves into the seams of the wing panels and crawled her way to the edge. She was bodily shaking and felt lightheaded. Sev looked down over the edge and spotted the ventilation duct beneath.

It was several feet away. She'd have to dangle off the wing and stretch to reach it. Her stomach roiled at the thought.

Sev crawled toward the drop-off; she grasped the edge of the wing with both hands, blew out a quick breath, and lowered herself down.

The split-second feeling of falling was the most terrifying moment of her life. When she came back to herself, she was breathing rapidly; there were spots in front of her eyes, and her hands were sweating inside her suit.

Sev hung on the edge, her legs dangling free in the great void of space for what seemed like an eternity. She knew, though, that she would have to reach her tool belt. She would have to free the duct. That would mean letting go and hanging on with just one hand.

She gritted her teeth, tightened her grip on the ledge with her right hand, and let go. Her stomach flipped; she reached the tool belt and withdrew the spanner in record time.

Sev grabbed the ledge again with both hands and sighed in relief. She eyed the duct where it tucked up against the side of the ship. It was a few feet away, but it might as well have been a mile. She'd have to swing to reach it, she realized with dread. Her arms ached.

Sev moved her legs back and forth, building momentum. She could feel her gloves slipping on the smooth surface of the wing, so she tightened her grip. Her fingers cramped, and pain shot down her arm. Sev stretched the spanner as far as she could reach it once, failed, and then swung herself out again. The tip of the spanner nudged the ventilation duct, but nothing more.

Her groan of frustration was deafening inside her helmet. *One more*, she thought, *one more time, Sev*. It grounded her…made her feel like her father was somewhere encouraging her success.

Then the ship canted. It threw her off balance, and she nearly lost her grip. *Am I losing control?* she wondered wildly, but there was no further movement. She closed her eyes, reaching out for Drek. Wishing for strength. Then the doubt crept in. *What if I can't do it? What if this is it?*

She gritted her teeth, willing those thoughts away. She wouldn't let all she had done be for nothing. Sev counted down from three, then swung out…she reached as far as she could. And her spanner sank into the duct.

Tears of joy stung her eyes. When she withdrew it, the spanner dislodged the obstruction and sent the space junk that had gotten trapped there spinning off into the Black. She'd done it. She felt queasy…elated. Her body was a jittery mass of nerves and relief.

Sev tucked the spanner away in her tool pouch and clutched the edge. With a massive amount of effort, she pulled herself up onto the wing, catching the edge with one knee and then the other.

For a moment she remained there, spread out on her back, catching her breath. Her arms felt like jelly from exertion; her legs tingled. She looked up at the star-dotted blanket of space, at far-off nebulae and the ochre pall of the solar storm, entranced by its beauty.

When she had caught her breath, she crawled across the wing to the open hatch. The cockpit would have to be repressurized, but all appeared well within. She got to her feet and took one last look into the rare and beautiful Black and stepped inside.

The hatch sealed with a hiss and a puff of cold. She repressurized the cabin, and when that was done, she put away her suit.

Sev sat down in the navigator's chair. She preferred it to her father's seat at the controls, although she was doing double duty now. That seemed like his spot, so she kept it for him.

She checked the course and made sure she was still on track. The console no longer flashed; no menacing alarms rang through the cockpit. All appeared to be well.

Sev relaxed, shaky and spent. Ocarro was just a day away, and she couldn't get there fast enough.

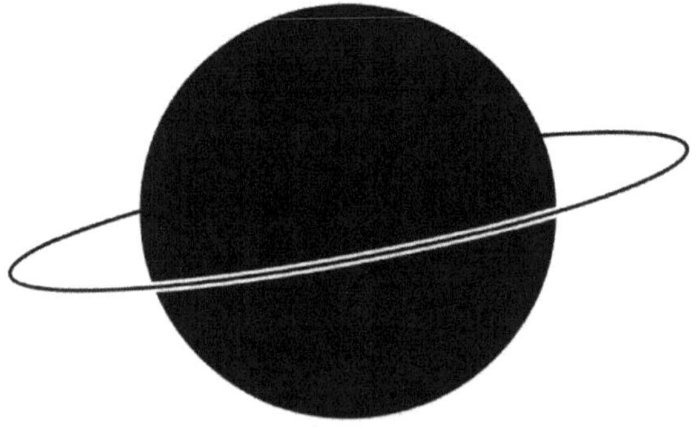

CHAPTER 28

Prescott eased into Phoenix's room. The lights were low; Pearla was asleep in the chair beside him, her head lolled against her shoulder.

He shook his head. She was wearing herself out, sitting with Phoenix. There was nothing she could do for him. He'd urged her to take lodging somewhere nearby, so she could come see him during the day. She'd refused.

He checked Phoenix's vitals and studied the latest sensor findings. It was subtle, but Phoenix was declining. His body was still rejecting the Lumiers, and the illness that brought him here was overtaking his immune system.

It wouldn't be long now.

He placed his hand on the man's arm, the skin fragile and dry. Soren had fought for Phoenix so desperately, had forfeited his freedom for him. But why?

Deep down, he knew. Phoenix reminded him of his mother, and Sev, himself.

Prescott remembered Soren as a young boy, maybe eleven or twelve. His mother had been gravely ill. The doctors met much like they had over Phoenix. Lumiers was the decided course of treatment.

Only it didn't work. Soren sat day in and day out, watching his mother waste away under the promise of a cure. Then, he wandered into his support group one day. He was so young. So scared. So full of fire.

Prescott took him under his wing. He tried to direct some of that passion and anger into medicine. But Soren's mother died. His father went to prison for being a dissenter not long after that. And Soren had no one.

He saw him through school, through university. Soren was a talented doctor, like he knew he would be, but that passion and fire remained. It made him reckless, a poor fit for Ocarri medicine.

Prescott had been wrong to push him. He knew that now. In another world, he would have a long and successful career being a healer. But on Ocarro? Well, Ocarri healers wanted things done a certain way, even if it challenged logic sometimes.

He shook his head. Across from him, Pearla stirred, waking up. She rubbed sleep from her eyes.

"Prescott? How—how is he?"

He paled. He wouldn't tell her the truth. Not now. It could harm the baby if she became too distraught, and he didn't want that on his conscience, too. One destroyed life was enough. Instead, he smiled. "I'm just checking some things," he deflected. Mercifully, she didn't press the issue.

He finished his rounds and headed out. Pearla caught his arm. "Can we talk?" She took a furtive glance at Phoenix. "Not here, though."

He led her across the hall to the waiting room. It was empty for now, affording them a few moments of privacy. They both sat on the couch there.

He held her hand, and she appeared grateful. "What's on your mind, Pearla? How can I help?"

Pearla looked down. Color tinted her cheeks, blush on her otherwise fair skin. She had the Ocarri coloring, in that way, but her striking blue hair and light eyes made it obvious she was an off-worlder.

"It's about the baby," she almost whispered, still obviously unsure of saying it aloud. "I was wondering, maybe, if I should tell Phoenix."

It touched Prescott deeply. *Tell him*, he wanted to say. *You won't get another chance*. But he didn't. He simply nodded.

"I think that's a fine idea, Pearla. It will give him a reason to fight. Or yet another. Between you and Sev, he's got plenty."

She smiled and looked away. "Phoenix is such an amazing father. He is so good to Sev. Kind, understanding. Giving. He'll be wonderful with the baby, I'm sure of it."

Prescott merely listened, holding her hand. "What about you?" he asked hesitantly. "Are you excited about the baby, Pearla?"

Tears welled in her eyes. She moved her hand to her stomach, then let it fall away. "I'm scared to death," she confessed. "I never thought about being a mother. And now with Phoenix sick, I keep thinking what if—"

She hastily wiped the tears that fell, and Prescott handed her a box of tissues. She mumbled her thanks. He looked at her sadly, wishing more than anything that there was something he could do.

"What if he doesn't make it?" she finished in a whisper. "What if I'm all alone?"

Prescott felt his throat growing tight. He knew she would likely raise that child she carried alone. Phoenix would never live to meet it, and it hurt him deeply.

"Pearla, my dear. What are you to Sev if not a type of mother? Do you not love her? Care for her needs? Are you not there for her when she needs a kind and listening ear? I hazard that you are more of a mother now than you realize."

Pearla couldn't suppress the smile his words wrought. "Do you think so?"

"I know so. And you'll be even more of one to this sweet babe." He sat back, considering. "Would you like to know the sex?"

She shook her head. "No, not without Phoenix."

Her refusal wounded him. He knew Phoenix wasn't likely to wake up.

Prescott managed a tight smile. "Ok. As you wish."

He realized then, although he couldn't bear to be so blunt with her about Phoenix's condition, that he needed to say something. "If you had to raise this baby alone, Pearla, I know you could do it. You are strong. Stronger than you realize. You would prevail."

It seemed to break her. Pearla sobbed softly into the tissue, and Prescott let her cry. He knew she realized what he was saying, in a roundabout way, and she was dealing with it as best she could.

She gathered herself and dotted her face with a clean tissue. "So, I should tell him?" she asked, but it sounded like more of a realization than anything else.

Prescott nodded. "Tell him, Pearla. While there's still time."

Her lip quivered, but she shed no more tears. "I better get back," she said. And he watched her go back into the room that was so familiar to her now, back to a man who was currently very far away.

Pearla walked back into the room, and Phoenix was unchanged. She liked to imagine that he had moved his hand, or a foot, but he had not. He remained unconscious, motionless, and very ill.

Prescott didn't want to tell her, but he didn't have to. Phoenix was worse. She had two eyes. She could see what was right in front of her.

Pearla sat down in the chair beside him and took his hand. "Phoenix?" She asked him. "If you can hear me, please give me a sign."

She looked at his face for any movement, any sign of awakening. His eyes moved rapidly behind the lids. His chest moved rhythmically, but it was too precise to be natural. She sighed, disappointed, but not surprised.

"I need to say something, Phoenix. And if I don't say it now, I'm never going to say it." She enfolded his hand with her own. "There's something you should know. Something unexpected has happened. Something wonderful." She took a breath, nerving herself. "We're going to have a baby, Phoenix. Can you believe it? A little baby. Sev will be a big sister."

It might've been her imagination, but she thought she felt his finger move slightly in her grasp. It gave her hope.

"I know we never talked about it," she said. "I know it's a surprise. But I hope that if you can hear me, wherever you are, that you're happy."

She pulled his hand up to her face and pressed her cheek against it. It was limp, but warm. "Come back to us, Phoenix," she pleaded with him. "This baby needs a father. And I need you. Sev needs you."

She thought of Sev, lost to her for as many days, with no way for Pearla to contact her. She sent up a prayer to Drek that Sev would make it back in time. Sev needed to see her father. And selfishly, Pearla needed her here when Phoenix's time came.

A tentative knock came at the door, and Pearla released Phoenix's hand. She looked through the large windows and saw that it was Fallon. She had a basket in her hand.

Pearla waved her in, and Fallon greeted her with a smile. "I thought we might have dinner together. When's the last time you had a home-cooked meal, hmm?"

Pearla huffed. "Oh, not since Dobani," she said. "But you didn't have to do all of this, Fallon."

Fallon was unpacking her basket on the table next to the bed. She had fresh bread, a hearty stew, and a bowl of chopped fruit. She simply shrugged. "What are friends for but to share a meal with? A little conversation."

Pearla smiled. The food smelled heavenly, and her stomach rumbled.

Fallon laughed. "See? Someone's hungry. Probably that little one. You've got to feed it, Pearla. You don't want a scrawny baby."

She shook her head, amused. Fallon certainly had a way with words. Pearla helped her arrange the food at the small table and took up a bowl.

Fallon looked at where Phoenix rested, silent and still beneath all the machines and sensors. "How's he doing?" she asked.

Pearla shook her head, but said nothing. Fallon didn't press. She understood, and that was enough.

"When my husband was bad, I don't think I left his side for a second. So, I know what you're going through, Pearla. And let me tell you, it may not seem like it now, but all this will be over one day. It won't last forever. But when you're in the thick of it, it sure seems like it."

Pearla took a spoonful of stew, blew on it, and took a bite. She nodded, chewing. The bread was fresh and flavorful. She pulled another chunk off and dipped it in her bowl. "It does seem like it will go on forever," Pearla mused. "But Sev will be back soon; I know it. And then everything will be better."

It felt like a lie, but after her low mood, she could use a little delusion.

"I can't thank you enough for this, Fallon. This is delicious."

Fallon smiled. "I'm so glad, hon. It's an old recipe from my home world. Good for the body and the spirit."

Pearla hummed. She could use all the help she could get now that she was eating for two.

CHAPTER 29

Soren watched the door, eyes fixed on the shaft of light that shone through the food slot there. Dust motes floated in its path, stirred by his breath.

He sat on the floor of the cell, his knees pulled up against the cold. There was no cot in solitary, no blanket for warmth. They pushed a sparse meal through the slot three times a day; he hadn't seen anyone.

Nor had he slept. He'd been in that position for hours…watching the door, clinging to the only light visible.

He knew this was his punishment for the fight. The bitter reality that it wasn't his fault, any of it, did little to help his feelings. It was dark in the cell, cold and damp. The stone floor was hard beneath him. The grit of the limestone walls dug into his back.

Soren wondered briefly if he'd had a worse day.

There was the crunch of boots on the sandy floor outside, the rattle of keys. The heavy metal door swung open, and two guards stood on either side of it.

Soren squinted at the sudden onslaught of light, blinding in its intensity. He blinked up at the two guards, trying to gauge why they were there.

"On your feet, 227. Time for your hearing."

His throat tightened. *Had it been two days already?* He'd lost track of time in solitary. He might've been there longer.

"Can I get cleaned up first?" His voice was raspy from disuse, and he was quite dirty.

One guard laughed. "After your hearing. No time now."

When he wasn't quick enough getting up, the guard reached and pulled him to his feet. His aching legs protested; he'd been sitting there for a while.

They shackled his feet and dragged him out into the hallway. It was warmer there, but that's where the comforts ended. The guards started walking, leading him and partially dragging him to the meeting room. Soren felt shame at his appearance, disheveled and unwashed as he was. He kept his head up, regardless. It wasn't his fault.

The guards arrived at the meeting room and entered without knocking. Five council members were sitting at a long wooden desk. The room was dimly lit and airish. Council members were having stim brew and chatting about Ocarri weather patterns. The forecast called for another blizzard. One councilwoman was concerned about the state of her garden.

They pushed him into a chair and went to stand by the door. It took a moment for the council to stop their banter, to assume some modicum of professionalism. Soren looked each of them in the eyes; if they were going to sentence him, they would have to remember his face.

"Prisoner 227," one of them began. "We have reviewed your file. You have been labeled a dissenter, and under Ocarri law, that comes with a stiff penalty." They shuffled some papers and consulted a holopad. "It says here that you were a medic at our esteemed Medical Center. It's unfortunate that you chose to break the rules so egregiously, putting lives at risk."

Soren clenched his teeth, and a muscle in his jaw twitched. *No one was put at risk by him releasing Sev. She was never even sick.*

He looked around…no one was there to stand with him. No representative, no friends or family. He was totally and utterly alone.

One of the council members yawned, then picked up a pen and started tapping it on the tabletop. His shiny rings flashed in the light. "It is by the authority of Ocarro that we hereby sentence you to death, at a date yet undetermined, in accordance with punishment for dissenters." He looked to his left, then right. "All in favor, say 'aye'."

"Aye," the other members said in unison, and Soren flinched at their combined voices. The lead council looked at the guards with thinly veiled disinterest. "You can take him away."

Soren sat reeling from the sentence. It was swift, merciless, and, most of all, unfair. "Wait," he said, "let me say something!" But they were already leading him out.

A guard jerked his arm roughly, the one he'd injured a few days before. "No reason to fight it. You should've thought of this when you broke the law."

The words felt like acid on his skin. Soren didn't feel like he'd done anything wrong. He followed his heart. He did what he felt was right, just like his mother had taught him.

They took him to the showers; they were empty this time of day, and he was glad. The guards afforded him no privacy as they ordered him to strip and stand under the cold spray.

Soren shivered, but not from the cold. He scrubbed away the days in solitary, but the film of what had just transpired lingered on his skin. He was going to die at the hands of the government. The only question that remained was when.

He pressed his head against the tiled wall of the shower stall, feeling faint. The cool tile grounded him. The water circled the drain near his feet, and he watched it swirl, then disappear. It felt like he was disappearing, his life slipping away right before his eyes.

"Times up," one guard informed him. It'd barely been five minutes.

He toweled off and put on a fresh jumpsuit. He was looking forward to breakfast, but they marched him to the Infirmary instead.

Jol was there, looking over some test results. He looked up when Soren entered, smiling broadly—but it faded almost instantly. Soren caught the quick flicker of change in his expression, the way his gaze swept over him. His damp hair, his slumped shoulders. He must've looked as bad as he felt.

"Where have you been?" he asked him. "I had your work detail transferred to the Infirmary three days ago."

Soren stood still as the guards unshackled his feet. "I've been in solitary," he said bitterly. "For the fight."

Jol narrowed his eyes. "You mean the fight you didn't start? That's a shame. I could've used you these last few days. It got hectic." He pointed to a stack of patient files spread over his desk. "You can start with those. Archive the files that aren't active patients and review the rest."

Soren hesitated, then made his way to the stack of folders. He worked quietly, only asking questions when it was necessary.

Jol put away his test results and walked over to him. He laid a hand on his shoulder. "What's happened, Soren? You're different today."

Soren's lip trembled, and he pulled it between his teeth to stop it. He couldn't thwart the rising emotion, though, or the tears he'd never allowed himself to shed ever since his incarceration.

"They had my hearing this morning," he said, his voice small. "They sentenced me to death, Jol. Death for what I did."

Jol gasped, then pulled him into a tight hug. "I'm so, so sorry, Soren. You don't deserve what's happening to you. And I would do anything to change it."

Soren nodded, wiping a few tears that had escaped his lashes. He withdrew and looked at Jol, black eyes glittering.

"How long do I have?"

Jol frowned and took a breath. "Could be tomorrow. Could be a year from now. No way to know." He looked at him piteously, and Soren could barely stand it. "I know that doesn't make you feel any better."

Soren quirked his mouth in a half-hearted smile. "No, it doesn't. But I've got today. That's something."

Jol smiled. "Let's get this paperwork done; then maybe we'll have some downtime."

They broke for lunch; Jol had an extra sandwich that he shared with Soren, and Soren was grateful. They were just finishing up when a guard appeared in the doorway. He had a prisoner in tow.

"This one is complaining of chest pains." He pushed him forward, and the prisoner nearly fell. "Probably faking it."

Soren stood and tenderly led him by the arm to a nearby exam table. He didn't recognize the man; he must've been from another cell block. Jol dismissed the guards and busied himself with restocking the supply closet.

"How long has this been going on?" Soren asked him.

The prisoner winced, his hand to his chest. "A few hours now," he said, obviously pained. "Started after breakfast."

Soren started his physical exam, keeping the prisoner talking to help him relax. "Breakfast, huh? Eat anything different? Other than our mess hall's finest?"

The prisoner huffed a laugh. "No," he said, wincing. "It hurts bad, though. Right here." He pointed to the area over his heart.

Soren activated a scanner and ran it over his body. He drew a blood sample and tested a strand of his hair.

Jol walked up to him. "What are we thinking?" he asked him. "Heart attack?"

Soren shook his head. "Blood is good. Levels are good. His heavy metals are up, though. I think he's been poisoned."

Jol raised his eyebrows. "How?" he asked. "All the food is regimented, and the guards watch the prisoners closely."

"The paint in the cells," Soren informed him. "It's toxic. I've been having headaches myself. You stay here long enough it can leach into your pores."

Jol looked impressed. He folded his arms over his chest and considered him. "Good work, Soren. Prepare the antidote. We'll let him stay for a few hours until it gets out of his system. I'll report this to the Director."

Soren smiled. Practicing medicine made him feel useful, something he hadn't felt since he'd arrived here. It made him feel alive. And for someone who had was just handed a death sentence, that was no small thing.

Later, after the prisoner recovered and went back to his cell, Jol approached Soren. "You're an excellent doctor, young man. I might've missed that. You didn't."

It pleased him. He stuck out his hand, and Jol took it. "I appreciate you letting me work here," he said. He looked down briefly, sadness dimming his eyes. "For however long I have left."

Jol hummed. "Well, I'm going to talk to the Director about your case. Maybe they can overturn it. Good doctors are hard to find…it would be a waste of talent and life for them to carry out your sentence."

That evening at the mess hall, he thought of what Jol said. Maybe he could help him, after all. Maybe the Director would listen.

Cyrus picked at his food, his mood low. He hadn't asked how the hearing had gone. He didn't have to. Word spread. Soren was a dead man walking.

"Is there anyone I can notify for you?" Cyrus asked him. "I get one call a month." He shrugged. "Special privileges for the long haulers." His smile was bittersweet.

It touched Soren that Cyrus would use his one call to notify someone of his death. Cyrus was a genuine friend if he ever had one.

After supper, he lay in his bunk, staring at the ceiling. Cyrus said nothing; he didn't have to. Soren could tell he was upset by his news. To have someone grieve with him was comforting, in a way, even if it was a silent understanding.

Soren thought of his mother. He wondered if she would be proud of him…of what he'd done in what little time he'd had here. She was gone so soon; sick when he was just a child, and dead not long after that. He wished they'd had more time.

His father was another matter. Soren and his father grew distant after the death of his mother. His father went to prison not long after; labeled a dissenter, he toiled in a work camp for the rest of life.

Soren felt the tears come, and he rolled over to face the wall. He would never have a wife…a family of his own. He came into this world alone, and he would go out the same way.

Despite the exhaustion of the last few days, sleep was elusive.

CHAPTER 30

The stark white orb that was the planet Ocarro shined like a beacon in a sea of black. Sev watched it in the view pane, growing larger by the moment.

She'd never been happier to see anything in her life.

After clearing the ventilation duct, her return trip had been uneventful. For the two days it'd taken her, she'd rested. She'd nibbled on ration bars. She'd thought of Phoenix.

Sev wondered how he was doing now, with so many days spent at the Medical Center. Surely, he was better than when she last saw him. It made no sense otherwise.

She thought of Soren. None of this would've been possible if it weren't for him. She couldn't wait to see him, to give him the spores. He would make the serum as promised; all would be alright, then.

In the view pane, Ocarro was so close she could make out the mountain ranges, the silver threads of rivers. She checked her fuel gauge; she had just enough to clear atmosphere, but it would be close.

Sev strapped in, switching over to manual control. She would save fuel that way. The controls protested being taken off autopilot, but she silenced the alarms. It was her turn to fly.

The ship flipped thrusters down, preparing for landing. Flames licked the side of the skiff, but their insulation was true; she and her father had fixed this old ship up well, and she would trust it to take her anywhere.

There was a great roar, and the entire ship shook. Sev nudged the thrusters, just a touch, redirecting her path to reentry.

They didn't respond.

She did it again. The thrusters roared, but no heat went to the engines. Her hands shook on the controls. Sev checked the gauges, and what she feared proved true: she was out of fuel.

The readout must've been incorrect before, and she had less than she thought. It was no matter…she was out now, and she had to deal with it.

She furrowed her brow, eyes on the control panel. She'd have to regulate the descent with grav inducers, which was risky at best. Sev pulled the lever, straining to keep it upright. It was heavy, and with the entire force of the ship behind it, it was fighting her at every move.

By degrees, the ship slowed until Sev could see white trees, frozen ponds. The landing pad for the Ocarro hangar was just below. If she could hold up the lever for a little while longer, the gravs would ensure a safe but rocky landing.

Her entire arm trembled with effort, but she kept the lever aloft. The ship rattled, and the engines groaned. The gravs softened the landing, but the force of the touchdown nearly knocked her from her seat, straps and all.

Sev slumped, completely drained. Her arm trembled from exertion, and her body thrummed with adrenaline. A landing was a landing, she thought wearily. She'd made it to Ocarro in one piece.

Sev took a moment to catch her breath. Her hands were still shaking, and she could feel her heartbeat pounding in her ears. When she felt steady enough, she unbuckled her straps and slid out of the seat.

The comms lit, and she answered the hail. "Unauthorized ship on landing pad 184, identify yourself," came a detached voice.

Her mouth quirked up in a smile. "I'm Sev," she said. "Fuel it up for me? I'll be back for it."

Sev could feel the shocked indignation over the comms. "Hey! You can't leave this hunk of junk here! This landing pad is for authorized transports only!"

She depressed the button on the comms with a wry grin. "Then authorize it."

Without another word, Sev hitched up her pack and left the skiff sitting on the landing pad, smoke billowing around it.

She hiked through the rough terrain until the medical center was in sight. Sev had no holopad with her, no way to call ahead. She only hoped Soren was there and ready to receive the spores.

Sev burst through the doors of the Ocarri Medical Center, the precious cargo she carried practically burning a hole through her pack. Within moments, an alarm blared, and security had surrounded her.

Past the security bots, Sev saw a team of doctors in hazmat suits racing toward her. There was nowhere for her to go. Nowhere to hide.

"I'll go willingly!" she cried with her hands held aloft. "But I must see Soren! Take me to Soren!"

They grabbed her on either side and began leading her down the hall. She kicked and thrashed. "Soren!" Sev yelled, struggling in their grasp. "I have them! I have the spores!"

She glimpsed Prescott standing at the end of the hall. His eyes were wide, his mouth parted slightly, stunned, as if he could scarcely believe what he was seeing.

Sev knew what he was thinking. She had done it. She'd gone to Terra Firma and made it back.

Prescott rushed to the scene, stopping Carlin where he and his team of doctors were escorting Sev to quarantine. "Let me talk to her," Prescott reasoned. "Please, Carlin."

Carlin frowned. "You have five minutes," he warned him, but Prescott only smiled.

Prescott dismissed the security bots and took Sev down a secluded hall. "Soren's not here, Sev," he whispered. "He's been arrested."

The words fell on her ears like poisoned rain. He was her only hope, and now he was gone. "For what?" she asked, her eyes wide in disbelief.

Prescott sighed. "For helping with your escape," he said.

Sev couldn't believe it. She remembered what he had said when she asked if he would get into trouble. *Only if I get caught.*

She swallowed, her mouth dry. "That's ridiculous," she said, seething. "Soren is a good man. He doesn't deserve this!"

Prescott nodded. "I don't disagree with you. But there's nothing to be done."

She met his eyes. "But I have the spores," she protested. "Can't you take them to him?"

Prescott shook his head. "No, Sev. Soren is off your father's case. I'm sorry."

Sev was heartbroken. Everything she'd done…all she had gone through had been for nothing. She shook her head in disbelief.

"I'm caring for him now," Prescott said with a prim upturn of his mouth. "You can give them to me."

A brilliant smile lit her face, and she wrapped her arms around his neck. "Oh, thank you! Thank you," she said, beaming. "Here," she said, pulling off her pack. "There in here."

She handed Prescott the tubes; inside, spores frothed an iridescent green.

He stared at them in wonder, holding them up to the light. Wordlessly, he put them in the pocket of his white coat.

"Endure the quarantine, Sev. When you test healthy, I'll make sure you get in to see your father. In the meantime," he said, patting his pocket, "I'll take care of things."

The security bots reappeared, and they led Sev away. She looked back at him, but rather than being upset, she was smiling.

Prescott walked back to his lab, his mind racing. There was much to do to get Phoenix well, but this was a step in the right direction.

That night, Prescott visited Sev himself and tested her blood. "So far, so good, young lady." He looked at her sympathetically. "Can I get you anything?"

She smiled. "My holopad? So that I can talk to Pearla?"

He nodded. "I think I can arrange that. Are you comfortable? Warm enough?"

She sat down on the cot, holding her arm where he'd just drawn the blood. "I'm fine. I'm just worried about my dad, is all. How is he?"

Prescott appeared thoughtful. "He's not doing well, Sev. I won't lie to you. Anyone who can fly a ship to Terra Firma and back deserves to be spoken to plainly."

Her eyes darkened. "Will he die?"

Prescott looked down, unable to meet her eyes. "If this serum doesn't work, he doesn't have long."

Sev put her head in her hands, running her hands over face. "Does Pearla know?"

He sighed. "I believe she suspects," he said. "I did not tell her outright for other reasons."

She looked at him curiously. "What other reasons?"

He slowly backed out of the room, eager to get to work. "Not for me to say. I must go now, Sev. There's much to do if we're going to get your father well again."

She held her hand up in farewell and stretched out on the cot. It was comfier than she remembered, or maybe she was just that worn out.

Sev thought of Soren, of the sacrifice he made. If her father lived, she would owe him a debt of gratitude. There was no way she would ever repay it.

The lights blinked out, and with the darkness came a wave of exhaustion. She was content now that her mission was over, and the serum was in the works. Quarantine was a small price to pay for that.

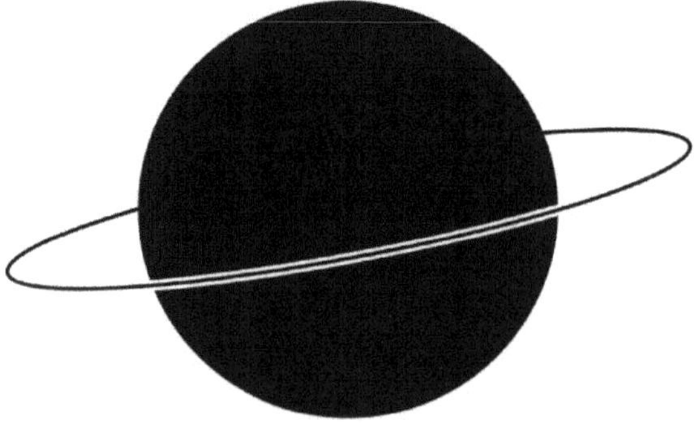

CHAPTER 31

The lab was cool and blessedly empty. Prescott could work in privacy, and that's exactly what he would need, coupled with a little luck, if he was going to make this serum.

He wore thick gloves and a protective suit. The spores bubbled when he added the solution; he aimed to stabilize them, to extract the protein and sterilize it. He was on the third try, and he was running out of spores.

The specimens were reaching the boiling point too quickly, spoiling his endeavors. He'd run out of ideas. He wished, above anything, that this was Soren doing this instead of him. Soren had better instincts, a knack for experimentation.

Prescott pushed away from the specimen, needing some air. He stripped off his hood and walked out into the hall. He desperately needed a stim stick, although he had quit years ago.

Prescott found himself in front of Sev's observation cell. He'd keyed in the security code before he could stop himself.

At the sound of the door opening, she looked that way. She was pacing back and forth, her holopad in her hand. She held it up.

"Did you do this?"

Prescott nodded.

She gave him a small smile. "Thanks," she said. "Still want out of here, though."

He walked toward her. "Should be soon, Sev. Your blood has tested clear since you arrived here."

She lowered her head, blowing out a frustrated breath. "Pearla said my dad is worse. That I need to see him."

Prescott watched as her gaze flickered over his suit. He didn't know what she was looking for, but he must've looked as frazzled as he felt.

"How's the serum coming?"

He shook his head. "I've spoiled three batches already, and I'm almost out of spores." He ran a gloved hand through his white hair. "I don't know what I'm doing wrong."

Sev inclined her head. He could almost hear the wheels in her mind turning. "What's the problem?"

He sighed. "It's boiling before I can purify it. I've adjusted the heat, added a binder. I am at a loss."

Prescott watched as Sev went quiet, her brow furrowing in deep concentration. She was working through something, mentally sorting through knowledge he couldn't see. Then, her expression shifted to recognition. A spark of realization.

"Add sugar," she blurted out. "It'll slow the boil long enough for you to purify it, and it won't change the chemical properties."

Prescott looked at her, appearing a little confounded. Then he hummed. "Yes, it could work. I will try again. I have enough for one more effort."

Sev approached him and put a hand on his arm. "You can do this," she told him. "I know you can."

He nodded. "I better go. They'll release you soon, Sev. I'm doing what I can. Stay strong."

He left her then, holding on to the belief that maybe, just maybe, she was right.

◆ ◆ ◆

Pearla sat by Phoenix's side. He had not changed in as many days. He still looked pallid, still looked thin despite the liquid nutrition that kept him fed.

Phoenix slept with only intermittent moments of lucidity. Pearla held her holopad. She was reading the Dobani news to him; she'd run out of things to say.

"Local weather fronts are balmy. Nights are cool with temperate days. Rain is expected on the weekend."

She looked at him for any sign of recognition. "Perfect weather for swimming before the rain comes, love. If we get home soon, we could go to the beach with Sev."

She frowned. They'd taken Sev into quarantine as soon as she'd returned, and she hadn't seen her. Pearla could scarcely believe she'd gone to Terra Firma and back with her safety and wellbeing intact. Sev was a remarkable girl. *Drek be praised.*

Pearla turned off the holopad. She stretched, weary from the all-too-familiar chair and her back aching.

Then, she felt something.

It was a tiny flutter, like bubbles. A strange sensation, akin to the wings of a butterfly. She put her hand over her belly. *Could this be the baby?*

She smiled. It happened again, stronger this time. It made her feel slightly queasy. She spread her fingers there, anxious for the day when she would feel stronger and more insistent movement. When she could share that moment with Phoenix.

"Oh, Phoenix," she said. "I can't wait for you to wake up." She clasped his hand and held it in hers. "Our baby," she said, her eyes watering. "It's the first time I've felt it."

Through the observation window, she saw Fallon. She gave her a cheerful wave and shouldered her way inside. She was carrying flowers.

"Thought it was time we brighten this place up a bit," she said. "How are you, hon? Eat today?"

Pearla smiled. "These are beautiful, Fallon. I visited the nutrition station earlier, so I'm good."

She remembered the sensation she'd felt. "I wanted to ask you. Earlier, I thought I felt something, Fallon. I think I felt the baby. Is it too soon? Is that a bad sign?"

Fallon laughed. "No, dear. It's a good sign. You are probably farther along than you thought." She inspected her critically. "You aren't showing yet, though. Still got that figure. How do Dobani women carry? Out front, like a beach ball? Or wide through the hips?"

Pearla laughed, her cheeks pinking. "I don't know, Fallon. All of this is new to me. I've never even had any pregnant friends."

Fallon tutted. "Well, I've carried three little ones myself, if that counts for anything. Are you still feeling sick?"

She shook her head. "No, that passed a bit ago. Now I'm starving."

Fallon grinned. "Then you should EAT," she said with a flourish. "You wait right here; I'll be right back."

Before Pearla could stop her, she was gone.

Moments later, Prescott rushed into the room. He was wearing his white coat and the same pristine white uniform Soren had worn. He was holding a syringe.

Pearl looked at him, her eyes wide. "Is that—"

"The serum," he said. "It's time."

Prescott sat in his spot by the window, sunlight streaming through the bars. A frozen lake surrounded the prison, making the austere complex even more foreboding. Even more bereft.

He looked up and Soren was walking towards him. The young man's hair was in disarray, and his shoulders were stooped. They'd shackled his ankles, as usual. Overkill for a nonviolent prisoner like him.

The guards sat him down opposite Prescott, and Soren held out his wrists. The guards shackled them to the table. *Again, overkill*, he thought.

"How are you?" Prescott said, not even letting the guards get out of earshot.

Soren quirked a smile. "Ok, for a dead man."

It wounded him. "You're not dead yet." He swallowed, a muscle in his jaw twitching. "I heard about the hearing. I wish I could've been there."

Soren shrugged. "'s ok," he said a little dismissively. "You're more useful practicing medicine. No need to put effort into those who are beyond help."

Prescott frowned. "Don't say that. I'm still advocating for your sentence to be commuted. I haven't given up hope, and neither should you."

Soren smiled sadly, but said nothing. The usual fire in his eyes had dimmed, some.

"What of Phoenix?"

Prescott leaned forward. "You won't believe what I'm about to tell you, but…the girl returned. She did it. She actually made it back."

A brilliant smile lit Soren's face, and he slapped the table with enthusiasm. "I knew it!" he tried to whisper. "I knew she could do it." Tears sprang to his eyes. "I knew it, Prescott."

"There's more, Soren. I made the serum. I administered it to Phoenix. It's done. Thanks to you."

Soren's eyes grew bright. "How is he?"

Prescott pressed his lips in a firm line. "It's hard to say. It's very early. The serum could take a week, maybe longer. But for now, he is unchanged."

It did not dampen Soren's spirit. "It's no matter. He'll live… I know it," he said. "I only wish I could've seen it through." His gaze dropped to the floor, his voice quieter now. "Thank you for telling me, Prescott. I can die a happy man now."

Prescott lay a hand on his arm. Soren may have resigned himself to die, but he wasn't ready to give him up just yet. "You'll stop talking like that in my presence, young man. If you know what's good for you." He looked at him sternly, yet his eyes were still tender. "This isn't over."

"Times up!"

They both watched as the guards approached. Soren gave him a sad smile. "Thank you," he mouthed. Prescott watched as they escorted him away, filled with renewed purpose.

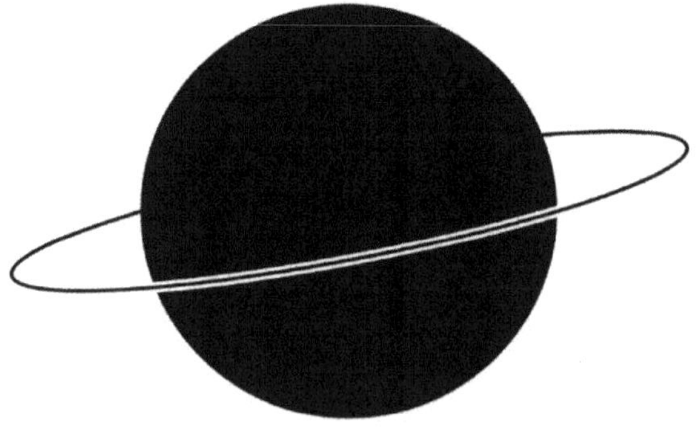

CHAPTER 32

The murky sunlight shone in water-filled potholes on the streets of Venya City. Phoenix walked along trash-strewn sidewalks, his hands in his pockets. He was 15 years old, lean and angry at the world.

Up ahead, there was another one. Tourists passing through Venya City on their way to tropical locales, somewhere with sunlit beaches and temperate water. They made easy marks. All he had to do was wait.

He ducked into the shadows, listening to their shoes on the sidewalk. This one was a woman, overdressed as usual, so hers were the clicky kind. He peeked out from the shadows. She wore a long fur coat and a sizeable strand of pearls.

He'd go for those first.

The woman passed the alley where Phoenix crouched, watching…waiting. He stepped out, a menacing sneer on his face. Phoenix held a blade, sharp and keen, but it was just to scare her, he told himself. He'd never even used it for more than scaling fish.

She screamed and turned to run away, but Phoenix caught her by the arm. He was young, but he was wiry and strong. She twisted in his grasp.

"Give me your card, and I won't stick you," he said menacingly. He nudged the tip of the knife upward. "The pearls, too."

The woman complied, her hands shaking. "You should be ashamed of yourself, young man. Robbing innocent people. As if this city wasn't wretched enough."

He pocketed the woman's card, then she handed him the pearls. "Maybe you're just unlucky," he shot back.

He released her and sprinted back down the alleyway. The woman screamed for help, for the Enforcers, but Phoenix knew they wouldn't come. Such was Venya City.

It was raining. Phoenix pulled his thin coat up over his head and ducked under a nearby fire escape. When he passed a scanner station, he checked the card.

Five credits. *We'll eat well tonight*, he thought. He shrugged his way out of his wet coat, and ducked onto the nearest transport, heading for home.

His mother was in bed, where she remained most days. White streaked her dark, lustrous hair. Her lips were pale and chapped. She saw him and smiled wanly, opening her thin arms to him.

"Sakes alive," she wheezed. "You're soaked to the bone!"

Phoenix shrugged. She started coughing, and he reached for the glass of water by her bed and brought it to her lips. "I'm fine, Mama. How do you feel, hmm? Any better?"

Cordera smiled weakly. "I'm ok, baby. But where have you been? I've been worried sick."

His eyes lit, and he pulled out the card. "Five credits Mama. We can get your medicine! And this."

He withdrew the strand of pearls from his pocket, and they gleamed in the low light.

His mother frowned, and Phoenix could see a dark realization pass over her face. "Phoenix, where did you get that?"

Phoenix gave her a lopsided grin. "It doesn't matter, Mama. Folks like her have plenty. She'll never miss it."

Cordera shut her eyes. A track of silver tears ran down her face. "Drek, have mercy on me," she whispered. "I never raised you to be a common thief. Phoenix, you are better than that."

He narrowed his eyes, his fist closing around the pearls. "Why should they have everything, Mama? When we go to bed hungry most nights?! It's not fair!"

Hot tears ran down his face, and he angrily wiped them away. "It's not fair! You're dyin', and there's nothing I can do!"

Cordera took her son in her arms and held her against him. "Shh, baby. Don't cry, now. We do alright." She rocked him gently as he sobbed. "I didn't raise you to hurt people, Feenie, my love."

Phoenix sniffed. "I'm sorry," he said against her, his voice muffled. "I didn't hurt her, Mama, I promise."

She patted his back. "Ok love…ok. You didn't hurt her. But what you did was still wrong. You understand?"

He nodded, still unable to look at her. "You go back to Venya City and give that woman her credits. And her necklace."

"But Mama—"

"Uh-uh, you do as I say," she said, as sternly as her weakened state would allow. "Go on, now. I'll scratch us up some dinner while you're gone."

He backed away. There was no way he would ever find that woman again; she'd been so terrified she probably got out of Venya City as fast as she could.

But he left, anyway. Phoenix took a transport to the Venya City Terminal. He sold the pearls at the exchange office; they fetched a handsome price.

He pocketed the money. He would have to be careful how he spent it, so his mother wouldn't find out.

The deception burned in his gut, but what was he to do?

Phoenix took the long transport home. When he arrived, his mother was at the kitchen table. She'd made bread with the last of the flour.

"Smells good, Mama. You didn't wear yourself out, did you?"

She smiled. "No baby. Your mama has some fight in her yet." She pinned him with a knowing glance, her eyes sharp. "Did you do as I told you?"

Phoenix gritted his teeth. His heart flipped with the magnitude of what he was about to do. He opened his mouth, half-hoping the truth would volunteer itself.

"Yes ma'am," he said instead.

Through the rain outside, he heard a faraway voice. It was a woman, pleasant and endearing. *"Phoenix? Honey?"*

Phoenix moaned, his eyes fluttering. Pearla sat up in her chair, looking over at him.

He moved his arm…it was the first time he'd been able to move it since the paralysis had struck, and he opened his eyes.

"I'm not the man I used to be, Pearla," he whispered brokenly.

She patted his hand, shushing him. "You don't have to tell me that, Phoenix. You're a good man. A good provider for your family."

A tear rolled down his cheek. "I wasn't always."

She smiled. "None of that matters now. How do you feel?"

His mouth quirked up into a smile. "Alive," he rasped.

She laughed. "Oh, wait 'till I tell Sev!"

Phoenix reached for her hand. "She's here?"

Pearla nodded. "Yes Phoenix. She made it back to you. To us. Everything is going to be fine now."

Phoenix blinked back tears. "I want to see her," he whispered.

A weight pressed against his hand—warm, steady. Fingers threading through his own.

His chest ached. Something was wrong. He exhaled, and for a long, heavy moment, nothing followed. No breath. Just stillness. Then, a sudden snap—his eyes clenched shut, his body locking tight as a surge of electricity raced through his limbs.

His world splintered. His arm and legs jerked outside of his control. A strange static haze filled his mind, sharp beeps piercing through it.

He heard a gasp, the chair scrub on the floor, toppling over, and Pearla rushing from the room.

CHAPTER 33

Prescott paced, nervous energy making him restless, the urgency of Phoenix's decline making him brave. "The girl's father is dying. She's not sick, Carlin. You have to release her."

Carlin scowled. "The only thing I *have* to do is follow Ocarri law. And that's what I'm doing."

Prescott stared him down. "If she tests clean by lunchtime, I'm letting her out. She needs to be with her father. So she can say goodbye."

Prescott walked down the hall and straight to Phoenix's room. It had all the somber stillness of a tomb, the tension of a held breath. He saw Pearla look up and follow him as he crossed to Phoenix's bedside.

Prescott looked down at him, reading the sensors. He was steadily declining; the hope he'd placed in the serum was sadly misplaced, and the seizure he had experienced recently only reinforced that. He dreaded telling Sev; he couldn't bear to think about what it would do to her.

"It's still early, though, right? I mean, the serum's still working, isn't it?"

He didn't want to tell her he thought it had failed, that Phoenix was at death's door, and he doubted anything could bring him back from the brink now. He simply nodded.

"We'll give him some nutrition, some medicines to keep him comfortable. Right now, it's just a waiting game to see if the serum has any effect."

Pearla inclined her head. He knew she could read between the lines of "keep him comfortable," and it was a bleak reality he hated she had to face.

"What about Sev? Her father needs her."

Prescott agreed. "I'm releasing her at noon," he said matter-of-factly. "She's not sick, not going to be sick. And you're right, Pearla. Her place is here."

She smiled. "Thank you for all you've done, Prescott. You've been so kind to Phoenix…and to me."

He looked away, then down at Phoenix. The man looked dead already, lying there tenuously clinging to life with whatever strength he had left. Whatever Prescott had done, it didn't feel like enough.

◆ ◆ ◆

Prescott stood outside the observation cell, looking in at Sev through the small window. He'd already risked so much for Sev and Phoenix—for Soren, too. Prescott did not have the reckless spirit that Soren had…the same rebellious passion did not course through his veins like it did Soren's. Prescott had worked to make a life here, a prestigious career. Did he really want to risk all of that?

He took a breath. There were worse things, he decided, than freeing a young woman who needed to be with her family. If Ocarri medicine thought not, then so be it.

He flexed his fingers, his hand hovering over the security panel. He took one more look at Sev, keyed in the code for the holding cell, and opened the door. Sev looked at him, alarmed, then curious. "Am I free to go?"

He looked at her, his face grim. "You are now."

She approached him, her arms crossed. "What's happened?" she asked him.

He didn't want to tell her like this, but the time for obfuscation had passed. "It's your father," he said. "It's near his time."

She looked down, and Prescott saw the grief settle over her like a shadow. She followed him down the hall, distracted. Sev was probably thinking about how the serum should have worked—after everything she'd done, everything she'd been through.

Prescott shook his head. In the end, it just wasn't enough.

Patient room doors stood open on either side, the beeps and clicks of machines bleeding into the hall. Up ahead, light streamed through a doorway, illuminating the polished floor. Prescott stopped, caught by some helpless curiosity.

Inside, a man sat up in bed, smiling. A woman leaned forward, wrapping her arms around him. A child, too young to understand the weight of this moment, lifted her hands for a hug, grinning wide. She had a red balloon tied to her wrist—a stark spot of color in the sterile, white hospital room.

People dying. People getting better. All under the same roof. The contrast made Prescott's stomach twist. It was dizzying. Claustrophobic. His hands curled into fists at his sides, and he forced them to relax.

When he glanced back, Sev was watching him, her expression unreadable. He ducked his head, quickening his pace. The foreboding of what he was about to see was almost overwhelming.

They approached the room and stepped inside.

◆ ◆ ◆

Pearla was there… sweet Pearla, with her kind face and long-suffering smile. She looked at Sev, her voice trembling as she tried not to break down.

"Oh, Sev," she whispered. "I knew you'd make it."

Sev ran to her, falling into her arms. Pearla smelled floral, like kinderbuds in spring. She smelled like coming home.

Pearla kissed her cheek, brushing her hair away from her face. For a moment she just looked at her, eyes roving over her face. "I just knew it with everything I had that you'd make it back," she said. "I knew it."

Sev withdrew, smiling. Pearla was not unchanged from when she left. Her eyes appeared sunken, with dark circles beneath. She was thinner, her face drawn. Pearla looked world weary. She looked tired.

Sev clasped her hand. "Thank you for your prayers," she whispered. "Everything is going to be okay, Pearla. You have to believe that."

Pearla's lips quivered. She looked as if she wanted to speak, but no words came. Her red-rimmed eyes shimmered with unshed tears.

Sev's stomach clenched. She didn't need Pearla to say it. She already knew. Nothing would be okay now. Her father was dying. He might not even wake up long enough for her to say goodbye.

But Pearla didn't speak those words aloud. Instead, she squeezed Sev's hand, her fingers trembling. A tear slipped down her cheek as she nodded, a silent confirmation that cut deeper than words ever could.

Sev studied her. Pearla looked devastated, but she didn't know Phoenix like Sev did. He'd come back from the brink before. He could do it again.

Sev turned to her father. He did not look the same as when she'd left. He was far worse…pale, wan, his legs too thin. Phoenix was but a shadow, now, of the man she knew.

"Daddy?" she said, her voice timid. "I'm here, Daddy. I came back like I said."

She sat down on the other side of him, her face painted green by the glow of the sensor screens. "Let me tell you about Terra Firma, Daddy. I know you want to hear how that old ball of trouble has changed."

She leaned in and kissed his cheek. "I handled the skiff fine…she flew admirably. You would've been so proud, Daddy, to see her cut across the stars. And Terra Firma…well, it's a different place now. Unrecognizable. The land has healed from the harvesting…it's a wild and brand-new world."

His hand twitched slightly. Could've been a reflex, or he could've been listening, trying to reach out. Whatever it was, the little sign of life encouraged her. She reached for it, pressing her hand to his.

"I know you're probably angry that I left you…that I went to Terra Firma alone. But I had to, Daddy. No one else could do it. I had to give you a fighting chance."

She leaned close to him, her brow furrowed. "So, fight, Daddy. Fight hard. Fight your way back to us."

The monitors tittered, but otherwise, he remained unchanged. Sev sat back, sad and deflated.

Pearla reached across Phoenix and took her hand.

"Sev, honey, while you were gone, I found out something amazing. Something unbelievable." She swallowed, looking unsure of herself.

Sev blinked at her, waiting for Pearla to find the words. She tried to read her face, to glean meaning from her body language, but she came up short.

"I really don't know how to say this...other than just to say it."

Sev held her breath, waiting. *Was it her father? Was there something about his condition that she didn't know? Something worse?*

"You're going to be a big sister, Sev." Pearla licked her lips nervously, her eyes flitting over Sev's face. "I'm going to have a baby."

Sev's eyes went wide, and her mouth fell open. For a moment, she said nothing, processing the news. Her mind raced—of all the things she'd expected Pearla to say, this had never crossed her mind. Her mouth went dry, and she promptly closed it. Pearla was watching her, waiting, nervous. Sev felt the weight of that expectancy, and she forced the shock to settle. She cleared her throat. "Drek be praised," she whispered. And then she smiled. "I can't believe it, Pearla. A baby?" She laughed. "And, you're sure?"

Pearla nodded. "Positive Sev. Our family is growing." She laid a hand on her belly, and Sev smiled at the unconscious action.

"Does dad know?"

Pearla looked a little downcast. "Not yet," she said, her voice hopeful, if not a little sad.

Sev nodded. "He will. You'll get to tell him yourself when he wakes up."

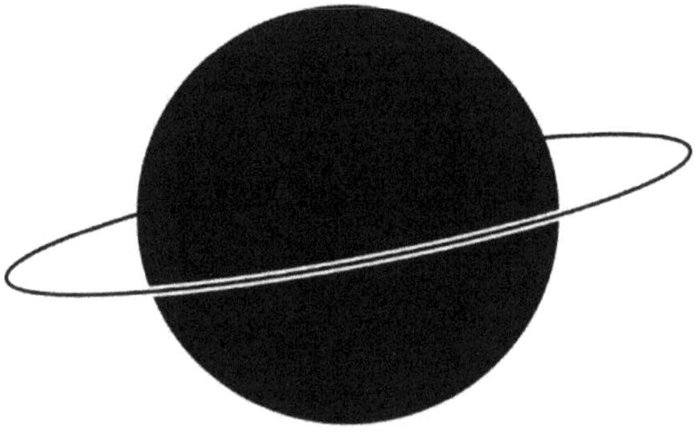

CHAPTER 34

Phoenix drifted. He knew he was dreaming; it was different now than before. Phoenix watched himself outside of his body. He was on Dobani. He was home.

"I hope you like pasta," Pearla said. The evening sun streamed through the small kitchen. It was warm and smelled of herbs, the spicy tang of red sauce. Phoenix looked and Sev was at the table…younger, just a child. Phoenix nodded. "I imagine I would like most anything you make, Pearla. That being said, this does smell delicious."

She smiled. Phoenix remembered this.

Pearla helped their plates, then brought a steaming loaf of savory bread to slice and serve alongside the meal. It was fragrant and fresh.

Phoenix blessed the food, thanked Drek for her provisions. He took a bite; flavor burst on his tongue.

"This is better than even what you make, Daddy," Sev said.

Pearla and Phoenix laughed. "I'm glad you think so, Sev," Pearla said, "but I'm sure your father's pasta is just fine."

Sev smiled around a mouthful of food, her green eyes alight with mirth. Phoenix reached for Pearla's hand, holding it affectionately. This was the first time in a long time his dreams hadn't been filled with ghosts.

He blinked, and he was still holding Pearla's hand, only he was not at home. The room was bright and stark white. It took a moment for his eyes to clear.

The ever-present pain in his head was finally gone. His body felt lighter, and he could feel his limbs.

Phoenix moved his fingers against hers, and she looked over at him. His mouth tugged into a weak smile. "Hey Pearl."

She huffed a relieved sort of laugh. His hand went up to touch her face, and she leaned into his touch.

Phoenix tutted. "Don't cry, now."

But tears spilled down her cheeks, anyway. Her shoulders shook, her breath hitching as if the weight of something had finally lifted.

"Where are we?"

She grabbed his hand. "We're on Ocarro. At the Medical Center. You've been so sick, Phoenix. I don't even know where to begin."

His eyes grew serious. He took in her bedraggled state; Pearla looked exhausted, worn out. But still beautiful.

"You don't have to," he whispered. "I see it in your eyes." He closed his. "I'm so sorry, Pearla, to have worried you so."

She smiled. "It's ok, love. You're here now, and that's all that matters."

The door opened, and Sev stepped inside, a cup of stim in her hands.

She stopped abruptly. Phoenix saw the way her body stiffened, the way her fingers curled tighter around the cup. Her eyes locked on him and Pearla, as if she couldn't quite believe what she was seeing.

Phoenix blinked up at her, offering a weak smile. His eyes burned—not from fever this time, but from the weight of everything left unspoken. He lifted his arm toward her.

"C'mere, little mouse," he said, his voice hoarse. "Let me see you."

Sev crossed the distance between them, hesitation in every step. Even without words, Phoenix could see the emotion tightening her features, the way her throat bobbed as if she were holding something back.

She eased into his arms, careful, as if afraid she might break him. Her head rested gingerly against his chest, her breath shuddering against him.

Phoenix exhaled slowly. He knew what she was feeling; he felt it, too. The steady rise and fall of his own breath, unassisted and free, felt like a miracle.

"I missed you, Daddy," Sev whispered tearfully, and he smoothed his hand over her back. "I didn't think you were going to make it. But I had faith…I had to have faith."

Phoenix shushed her. "I'm right here, mouse. I'm not going anywhere. You know it will take more to get me down than a little headache now."

Pearla sighed, and Sev looked at her knowingly. Sev withdrew so she could look at him fully.

"You have no idea, do you Dad?"

Phoenix only looked at her, perplexed.

Sev settled in the chair opposite Pearla. "You were spore sick, Daddy. You nearly died."

Pearla sat up, placing a hand on his arm. "Sev flew to Terra Firma to bring back spores for your cure."

Phoenix looked on, his mouth agape. "Terra Firma? Mouse? Why didn't you tell me?" He reached out and placed his hand on her arm, giving it a desperate squeeze. "If something would've happened to you—"

"It didn't, Daddy. I made it back. And you're better, now. That's all that matters."

Sev hugged her father, and he threaded his fingers through her hair. It was all he could think about. The reality of almost losing his life, Sev's life, weighed heavily on him.

He looked up, and he saw a doctor watching them through the windows. He was staring at him, a disbelieving smile on his face. With a beckoning motion, he welcomed him in.

Prescott eased into the room, his hand in his pocket. He approached the bed where Phoenix lounged with his family sitting around him.

Prescott stuck out his hand. "It's a pleasure to meet you, Mr. Phoenix. My name is Prescott. I'm in charge of your care."

Phoenix shook his hand, his mouth crooking into a smile. "You saved my life, Doc. That's no small thing."

Prescott shook his head. "Your daughter saved your life, Phoenix. Sev is a remarkable girl. But I think you already know that."

Phoenix smiled fondly, tears springing to his eyes. "I do indeed, Doc. She's the rarest jewel I ever found."

Sev's lips curved into a smile, clearly catching his meaning. She was his most valuable find on Terra Firma. His truest treasure.

As he looked at her, something shifted in her expression…relief, maybe, or something deeper. Phoenix wasn't sure. But the way her shoulders eased, the way her grip on his hand lingered, told him everything he needed to know.

She'd missed him. And he was finally here.

Prescott nodded to Pearla. "Have you told him yet, Pearla?"

It immediately got Phoenix's attention. He looked at Pearla and she had a surprised, almost hesitant look on her face. "No," she conceded, waving it off. "Not yet."

"Tell me what, Pearl? Is there something wrong?"

Sev pressed her lips together. She looked at Pearla. "I think I'm going to step out for some air," Sev said. Phoenix looked at her curiously. Prescott followed her out. He and Pearla were alone.

"What's going on, Pearla? There's something you're not telling me. Don't worry me, now."

She shook her head. "Nothing's wrong, hon. But there is something you should know."

Phoenix watched her, trying to read her intentions. He could tell she was nervous, the way she was waffling. He reached out and caressed her face.

"You can tell me anything, Pearla. You know that, right?"

Pearla smiled, and Phoenix took in the quiet around them. The rhythmic hum of machines, the beeping monitors—they were gone. Disconnected the day before.

They hadn't expected him to make it. He could see it in Pearla's eyes, in the way she looked at him like he was a miracle she hadn't dared to hope for.

A gust of wind rattled the walls, and Pearla's gaze drifted toward the window. Phoenix followed her stare, knowing she was thinking about the cold outside, the snow stretching endlessly beyond these walls.

She licked her lips nervously. "You know I love you, right? And I love how you love…fiercely and without restraint. You'd do anything for Sev; one of the first things that attracted me to you was how much you love her."

He nodded, not knowing where this was going, but needing her to continue.

"And I know, if we ever had someone else come into our family…I know you would love them, too. "

He smiled. "Of course, Pearl, but what are you—"

"We're having a baby, Phoenix."

Phoenix stared at her, in visible shock. His heart beat wildly; his breath caught. "A baby?" he stammered, unable to believe what he was hearing. "You're saying I'm going to be a daddy?"

His hand shook, and he raised it to his mouth. Pearla laid her hand against him. "Yes, Phoenix. You're going to be a daddy yet again." She looked at him, visibly apprehensive. "Are you happy?"

His eyes filled with tears. What if he had died? he thought. If he hadn't made it, Pearla would've had to raise this baby without him.

"C'mere," he said. He met her halfway, kissing her deeply. "I'm so happy, Pearla. You've made me so unbelievably happy."

He withdrew, his eyes warm. "Does Sev know?"

Pearla nodded, resting her forehead against his. "She's excited. She can scarcely wait."

As if summoned, Sev opened the door, peeking her head through. Phoenix saw her questioning glance and smiled.

"So, what do you think?" she asked him.

He laughed. "I think I'll have two little jewels to look after soon."

He looked at Pearla, his eyes still damp with tears, his chest aching—not with pain, but with something deeper. Something full.

Outside, the wind had died down. Sunlight streamed through the only window in his room, casting a golden glow across the bed.

Sev stepped closer, reaching across him to take Pearla's hand, framing him in warmth. Phoenix smiled, his throat tightening. They were a family again. Whole. Complete. And growing.

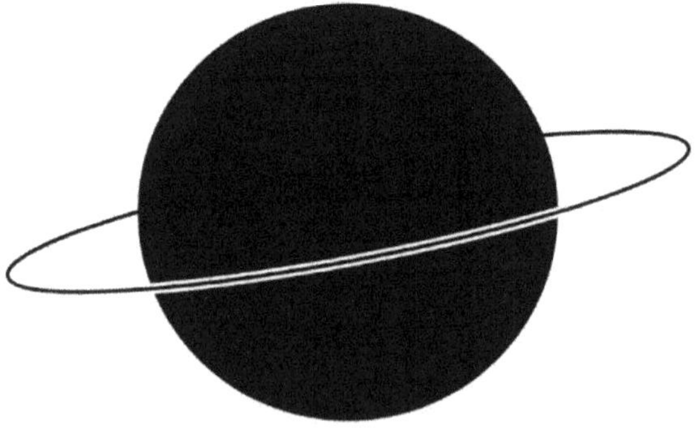

CHAPTER 35

The next morning, Phoenix sat up in bed. He wore a fresh medical tunic, and his hair was still wet from the shower. He had a simple breakfast of porridge in front of him. Sev watched her father eat with his one hand, the spoon a little unsteady on its way to his mouth.

Her father was better…thriving even, given the grave state he'd been in. She had all she ever wanted. But her heart was unsettled.

Soren never got his happy ending, and if it wasn't for him, none of this would be possible.

She looked up at her father again. He was halfway through the bowl, but not likely to finish it. He reclined against the pillow, his eyes closed. "Still pretty tired," he said. Then he smiled. "But better."

Sev couldn't help but smile back. "You'll get there, Daddy. It's gonna take time."

He nodded. "Indeed, little mouse." He brushed his damp hair back over his head, his gaze settling on her. She could feel the weight of it, how he saw right through her distant demeanor.

"What's on your mind, love? And don't tell me nothing." He grinned. "No use lying to your old man."

She sighed. "There's a guy…an Ocarri medic."

Phoenix's eyebrows lifted. "A guy, huh? Well, if he's got you so glum, he may not be right for you, Sev."

She blushed at the misunderstanding. "No, Dad. It's not like that. He's the reason I knew you needed spores. He's the reason you're alive as much as I am."

Phoenix eyed her. "Then fetch him, sweetheart, so I can thank him properly. Where is he?"

She bowed her head. "He got in trouble for helping me. He's in prison."

Phoenix whistled long and low. "You better go to him, mouse. If he saved my life, he deserves to know he matters."

She knew her father was right. Soren needed someone; now that her father was better, she could visit him, see how he was doing.

"You'll be ok here? Where's Pearla?"

Phoenix smiled. "Pearla is catching a nap. I insisted. Poor thing is worried out. She'll be back soon."

He motioned her out the door. "Go, Sev. I'll be fine."

She nodded and stood to leave. Sev was halfway to the door when her father called her. She turned around."

"I love you Sev. For all time. I didn't want you to think…with the new baby and all…that—"

She couldn't suppress a smile before holding up her hand. "No, Daddy. I would never think that. And I love you too. So much."

She took a last look at him in the hospital bed. His color was better. He was reclining on a pillow, looking out the window. He seemed at peace. Healing.

He was right, of course. She needed to see Soren, if only for herself.

♦ ♦ ♦

She hailed a transport, which, on Ocarro, was a completely new experience. Because of the terrain and the snow, the transports were large, lumbering land-bound vehicles with thick treads. The ride was rough and slow. It gave her time to think.

Sev went over what she would say to Soren, rehearsing it in her mind over and over. "Thank you for saving my father's life" seemed trite, considering his imprisonment. "I'm sorry I ruined your career and basically your life" wasn't appropriate either.

She huffed, frustrated, and placed her head against the view pane. It was cold, like the entire planet. She'd be so happy to leave.

After a few slow hours of tedious travel, the prison came into view. It was a sprawling, severe-looking building surrounded by a frozen lake. Its slate-gray walls blended into the snowy sky, making the building appear to go on forever. There were only a few windows, and they stood barred and heavily guarded.

She swallowed. This was the first time she'd been to such a place, and she was a little apprehensive about what all was waiting within. A lot of the people here deserved to be here, unlike Soren. A little jolt of nerves went through her at the thought.

The transport dropped her off at the front gate. She made her way through the security checkpoints systematically; they scanned her body multiple times and searched her belongings. Finally, they gave her the all-clear, issued her a visitor's badge, and sent her to a small room.

It was cozy in a claustrophobic and dated sort of way. A small couch and two chairs took up most of the room. There was a lamp and a potted plant. Ocarri people liked those, she surmised, from the number of them in the medical center waiting room.

She sat down on the couch and waited.

It was nearly an hour later when the door opened. It was Soren, with two guards on either side of him.

They led him inside. She looked down and there were shackles around his ankles. "You have twenty minutes," one guard informed her.

She stood to meet him in the middle of the room. He had his head down. His hand was in a cast. She reached out and tipped his chin up with her hand so he would look at her. So far, he had not.

His eyes were lifeless, like all the hope and joy had been drained away. "What happened to your hand?"

He frowned, perhaps hesitant to tell her. "I hit someone," he mumbled. "Broke a few knuckles."

Sev pulled her hand away, unconsciously recoiling. He quirked his mouth. "It's not like that. It's not how it seems."

She turned and walked toward the couch, patting the seat beside her. "Tell me how it is, then."

He followed her to the couch and sat down. He looked at her then, and something in his expression shifted, like he was taking her in for the first time. His eyes lingered on hers, warmer than before, but still unreadable. Still bereft of joy.

"I'd rather not talk about it," he said instead.

She nodded. "Can I give you a hug?" she asked tentatively. "I feel you could use one. To be honest, so could I."

He smiled, and she took him in her arms.

He was stiff at first, as cold and as sterile as the prison, but by degrees, he melted against her. A long, decompressing sigh escaped his lips, and he relaxed. Sev felt the warmth between them, and she thought of Dobani, of home, and wondered if he was thinking of somewhere else, too.

He withdrew first. "I guess you heard by now," he said, averting his gaze.

She bowed her head, lest her eyes betray the pity she felt for him. "Prescott told me."

"Hmm. I figured. At least they give you this nice room to meet in, though. And five extra minutes. Benefits of a death sentence, I guess."

The joke fell flat, and he shrugged his shoulders.

Sev frowned. "Prescott is fighting for you, and now, so am I. I'll talk to whatever office I have to. I won't forget you, Soren."

He smiled. "I will never forget you, Sev. Not if they kill me a hundred years from now. Not a chance."

Her throat grew tight. She remembered what she came here for…but that wasn't all.

"My father is getting better. All thanks to you. You saved his life, Soren. You did that."

Soren shook his head. "I just came up with the idea. You made it happen, Sev."

She blinked, and she could see herself in the black mirrored depths of his eyes. "I don't know what I would've done now, had I known what would happen."

His mouth turned up in a smile. "You would've done the very same thing. That's just who you are."

She looked away, abashed. He reached out and nudged her head back so he could see her properly, the pads of his fingers cool against her cheek. "Hey, that's not a bad thing."

The door opened. Light streamed in from the dusty hall. "Times up," the guard told them.

Sev looked at him, panic coursing through her veins. Would this be the last time she ever saw him? she wondered. *Most likely.*

Soren grabbed her hand. "Think of me often," he whispered.

The guards clutched his arms and hauled him to his feet. He was halfway to the door when the shock of his departure finally wore off. "Always, Soren," she said after him.

The door shut with finality, leaving her alone.

"Always," she whispered.

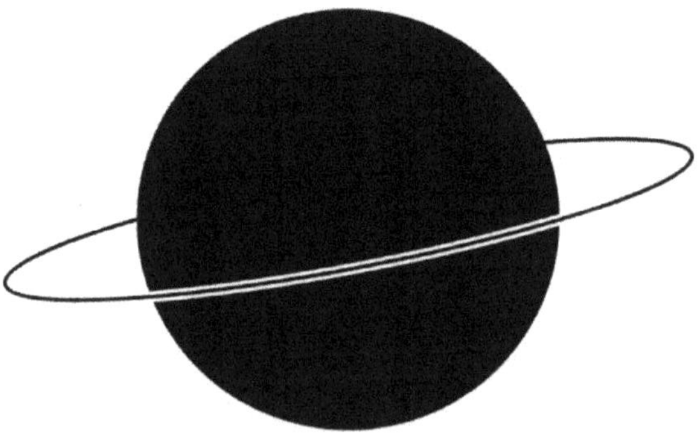

Phoenix sat on the edge of the bed, working his ankle up and down. It felt strange, being up again, being awake. The dreams of his illness still haunted him, the ghost of their memories lingering in his mind.

Pearla watched off to the side, her arms folded. The therapist held his hand, steadying his other side, and pulled him to his feet.

Phoenix stood, a little wobbly at first but finally firm, grounded. He took a step and the Ocarri therapist tutted. "Too soon, Mr. Phoenix. Stand a moment and get oriented. And straighten your back." They pulled on a belt around his middle, emphasizing the point.

He stood up straight, mindful of his posture. The room swam, and he shut his eyes. "Just a mite dizzy," he said. "Give me a moment."

The therapist smiled. She was young, with short black hair and pale skin common to the Ocarri. "It's normal," she told Pearla. "He's doing great."

Phoenix took a breath, then let it out slowly. His first step was steady, then the next. With the therapist's guidance, he'd walked across the floor in no time.

She sat him on the edge of his bed and disappeared for a moment. When she returned, she was rolling in a large, comfortable looking chair. "No more bed for you, Mr. Phoenix. Return to bed only for sleeping."

He smiled. "That I can handle," he said. "About time I was up and moving around."

She stood him up and led him to the chair. "I agree," she said. "The quicker you're walking on your own, the quicker you get to go home."

The word "home" resonated. Unbidden, images of their little house by the sea came rushing back. What he wouldn't give to be there right now, on his couch or at his desk. He had to resume his studies as soon as possible. And there was much to do before the baby.

He shook off his fantasy, and the therapist was standing with Pearla. "Call me if you need anything," she said.

The door shut, and they were alone.

Pearla looked at him, beaming. "Just look at you," she said. "Prescott says it won't be long. We can head for Dobani."

He grinned. "Ah, Pearl, I can scarcely wait." She sat on the edge of his bed, facing him. He appraised her curiously. "How do you feel? Any movement?"

She laughed. "Not today. You'll be the first to know, hon. I've only felt them once. But Prescott said that's normal, it being so early."

He nodded. The therapist had adjusted his chair, elevating his feet. He closed his eyes. For the first time in a while, he was quite comfortable.

Behind his lids, his dreams resurfaced. His eyes flew open, and he swallowed.

Maybe talking it out would squelch them for good, he thought. He did not want to forget outright, but he didn't want to be plagued with memories, either. Life was for the living, not dwelling in the past.

"Pearl," he began. "Did I ever tell you about my brother?"

She shook her head. "No, Phoenix. I didn't know you had one. But tell me."

His mouth quirked in a smile. "I dreamed of him while I was ill. So many times. His name was Lorien. He was younger. Sweeter. More everything than me. Everyone cherished him."

Pearla smiled. "Certainly not sweeter, Phoenix."

He huffed a laugh. "Indeed, Pearla. He was very special."

Pearla leaned forward, her expression open, searching. She wasn't just listening, she was absorbing every word, waiting, willing him to say more.

◆ ◆ ◆

They released him on a Tuesday. After so long at the medical center, they really hadn't acquired anything, having come there with just the clothes on their backs. The packing was light. Still, Sev fussed.

Sev watched as Phoenix shrugged into the fresh shirt she and Pearla had gotten him, the new pants. He wouldn't go home in a medical tunic, not in the Ocarro snow.

"Will be glad to get back to my arm," Phoenix grumbled. "Not as handy with just the one as I used to be. Isn't that right, Sev?"

She smiled. "I remember when you could gut a fish in three seconds flat with just the one," she mused.

He laughed. "Aye, you remember right. My prosthetic has made me lazy, but I've earned a little laziness, I think."

Pearla moved to face him, straightening his collar. "You have, my dear. And you aren't going to overwork yourself when we get home, either. Sev and I will see to that."

"Right," Sev agreed. "You're going to take it easy."

Phoenix smirked. "No such thing. Indeed, Doc has given me a clean bill of health." He spied him through the window right before he entered the room. "Isn't that right, Doc?"

Prescott entered, his hands folded in front him. "I seem to have missed the punchline."

It drew a hearty laugh from Phoenix. "I was just saying as how you had given me a clean bill of health. No need to rest."

Prescott smiled, indulgent. "Well, now I didn't say there wasn't a need to rest, but you can return to normal activities. Within reason, Phoenix."

Phoenix nodded. He stuck out his hand for Prescott to take, and the man shook it. "Thank you, Doc, for everything. For taking care of Pearla, besides."

Prescott hummed. "It was my pleasure, Phoenix. I couldn't have asked for a better outcome." He looked at Sev fondly. "Let's just say it was a group effort."

There was a tentative knock on the door. It opened a crack, and a thin face appeared in the space. It was Fallon.

A brilliant smile lit Pearla's face. "Please come in, Fallon. Meet Phoenix and Sev."

Prescott took his leave, and Fallon edged inside, looking around shyly. Her eyes fell on Sev first, where she packed and repacked their small bag. "So, this is who I've heard so much about." She pulled her into a quick hug. "She's a beauty, Pearla. You didn't say."

Sev blushed, somewhat abashed by the praise. Phoenix cleared his throat. "She's the apple of her daddy's eye, that one. You're Pearla's friend, right?"

She hugged Phoenix then, fond and warm. "That's right, Phoenix. And you're looking dashing, I must say. And very well. Going home today?"

"The very day," he said proudly. She got to Pearla and hugged her, too. Their embrace lingered. "I'm going to miss you," she whispered. "But I'm so happy for you."

Pearla withdrew, holding her friend's arms. "We'll keep in touch," she said. "You'll let me know about your husband."

Fallon smiled. "Of course I will." She leaned in and gave Pearla a peck on the cheek. "This is 'see you later', not 'goodbye'." Pearla nodded; her eyes misted with tears. She held Fallon's hand for several seconds.

Sev checked her holopad and looked up at both Pearla and her father. "The transport is ready," she said with an exhilarated smile. "Time to go."

The transport took them to the landing pad. Phoenix gabbed the whole way.

"I still can't believe it, little mouse. You took the ol' skiff to Terra Firma and back without me. In all my days…"

Sev smiled to herself. Her father's grumbling only reminded her he was better now. Things were back as they should be.

They arrived at the landing pad and boarded the skiff. Phoenix boarded first and was sitting at the controls when Sev and Pearla climbed inside.

Sev smiled. "Don't think so, Mister. You're still recovering," she said as she shooed him away. "Besides," she said with a smirk. "I like to drive, despite not knowing how."

He huffed. Pearla smiled. "I guess you'll be wantin' your own transport after this," Phoenix said, mock frustration tinting the humor in his voice.

Sev pretended to consider. "A convertible, I think. Red? Maybe blue, like the skiff."

Phoenix shook his head. Sev readied the controls, and the thrusters fired. "Strap in, you two. We're going home."

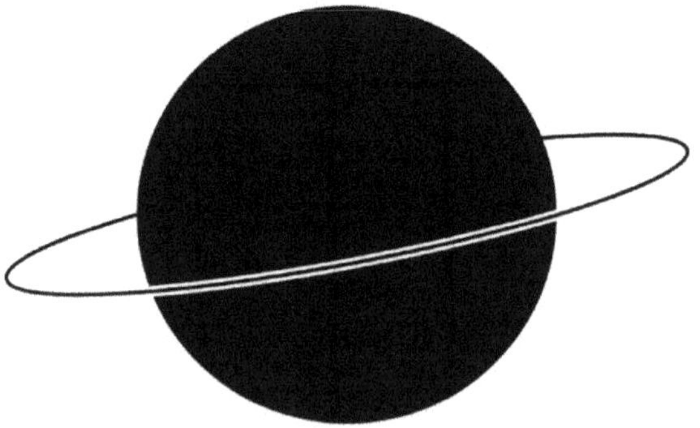

CHAPTER 37

They touched down on Dobani soil, and Phoenix could feel it in his bones. The trip was a good one, no issues. His little mouse was quite the pilot, but he knew that already.

They hailed a transport at the hangar, and Phoenix couldn't stop looking around, breathing the briny air. Pearla slipped her hand in his. "You ok hon? Need to sit down?"

He shook his head. "I'm just fine, love. More than."

Sev stood looking out at the flat expanse of land surrounding the hangar, and beyond that, Dobani Proper. Her father called her, and she turned around.

"It's good to be home, isn't it, mouse?"

She smiled. "More than, Daddy. I have everything I ever wanted. We're all together. We finally made it."

He blinked back tears. She'd done so much, risked her life so that he might be well. He only hoped he was the kind of father she deserved.

The transport arrived, and they strapped in. The ride was a lengthy one, but none of them were impatient. Phoenix gazed out of the view pane, watching the landscape change, staring wistfully at the silver thread of the ocean just beyond the dunes. He was quiet. They all were. The exhaustion of the last days had finally sunk in.

They turned down the sandy path to their house. Phoenix spied the stubby grasses, the stalworth grove of palms. He stepped out into their yard; Sev and Pearla quickly joined him.

The three of them stood looking at the little house, half afraid that if they blinked, it might disappear, a mirage in the sand. Sev put an arm around her father. "Let's go in, Daddy. You need to rest."

He didn't mind the fussing; he knew it was a manifestation of Sev and Pearla's love. But he felt more than capable…he felt fit, better than he had felt in a long time.

Phoenix never said as much. He followed them into the house and through the door, eager to see it.

The house stood scattered and in disarray. Sev paled. "I'm sorry, Daddy. I was in quite the rush, and it took some hunting to find what I needed."

He smiled. "Don't think on it, little mouse. The house can be put right again with just a little effort."

Pearla led Phoenix by the hand. "To the couch. I'll make us something to eat. You're too thin as it is."

Phoenix chuckled. "It didn't hurt me to lose a few pounds," he said with a grin. "But I won't turn down your cooking."

Sev smiled and began straightening the house. Pearla hummed, taking up residence in the kitchen. Phoenix dozed, despite saying he wasn't tired. He dreamed of the house set right, of the baby and a beautiful nursery. They were together. Everything was right and well for the first time in a long time.

◆ ◆ ◆

After supper, Sev kissed her father's cheek. "I've got somewhere I've gotta be, Daddy. But I'll be back soon. I promise." She looked up at him, questioning. "Do you mind if I take the transport? I'll be careful."

Phoenix considered. She'd piloted the skiff with aplomb. She'd proven herself trustworthy and capable, besides. He nodded. "Take it, dear heart. Watch out on the road. And be back before dark."

She hugged him, thankful for his trust. "I will," she said.

Sev drove the transport to the junkyard. It was quiet among the monoliths of old engines, transport parts, and the rusty husks of ships. She parked the transport and walked the trail to Uncle Dak's house. His piece of calcet felt heavy in her pack. The sooner she made good on her bargain, the better she would feel.

She knocked on the door, tentatively at first, then louder. She could hear Dak grumbling within. "Who at this forsaken time of the day…don't you know you don't call on someone so late…"

The door swung open, and once he saw who it was, his eyes softened. "Well, as I live and breathe. You made it, huh, kid?"

Sev smiled. "Did you have any doubt?"

He grunted. "Some," he admitted. "Come in then. I was just sitting down to chow."

She followed Uncle Dak deeper into his homie dwelling. Indeed, his plate sat fixed at the table, still steaming.

"I won't be long. Don't want to interrupt. I just wanted to bring you something."

Dak frowned. "Grab a plate, will ya? There's plenty."

She politely declined. "Already eaten, Uncle." He sat back down at the table, and she fished around in her pack until she found the calcet. She closed her fist around it and brought it out into the light.

The piece of calcet was as blue and beautiful as the day she found it in the sacred cave…a rare thing. She was so thankful for the Verdani's gift of it.

She shrugged, suddenly shy. "I'm sorry there aren't two of them. This was all that's left. You were right, Uncle Dak. Terra Firma is a wild, untamed place. All the calcet was gone."

Dak whistled, his eyes wide. "That's a pretty thing; never seen a blue one."

She smiled. "It's rare, for sure." She did not mention how sacred it was, or what it meant. Doing so would require her to reveal the Verdani, something she swore she would never do.

Dak took the calcet, turning it in the light. His lips pressed together, unreadable, before he finally looked away and handed it back to her. "You keep it," he said, his voice gruff.

Sev's hand wavered where he'd place it in her palm. "Why? It's your payment. I'm as good as my word."

He snorted, then took a bite of his food. "I said I don't want it, little lady."

She frowned and withdrew her hand. She slipped the calcet back into her pack. Sev stood there in front of Uncle Dak, a little lost for words.

"I also wanted to say thank you, Uncle Dak. You really saved my life out there. The suit was true. The filter was good. I couldn't have saved my dad without you."

He grunted. He looked up at her, the spoon poised near his mouth. "Food's getting cold."

Her shoulders dropped a little. "I'll let you eat, then." She backed away toward the door. "I'll check on you from time to time, if that's ok."

He hummed, still chewing. "Fine."

She might've imagined it, but Sev caught the hint of a smile on his face before it faded completely.

Sev left Uncle Dak to his supper and walked back to the transport. She felt accomplished. She felt free.

When she returned home, the house was quiet. It wasn't the unnatural quiet it had been when she had first returned from Ocarro; indeed, it was a peaceful silence. The house felt full again.

She saw Pearla in the kitchen, stirring a cup of tea. "Hi, Sev," she beamed. "Take care of your business?"

Sev nodded. "Could you tell Daddy I'm home? I know he was worried."

Pearla smiled. "Your father's asleep, but I'll tell him when he wakes up. He's more tired than he lets on."

"You are too," Sev said. "You didn't get much sleep at the Medical Center, and you need it, Pearla. For the baby too."

She sipped her tea. "You're right, of course. But I feel restless. It's like my body doesn't know everything's ok, now."

It made a peculiar sort of sense to Sev. "I'll sit with you awhile; maybe you'll get sleepy," she offered, and Pearla smiled.

Pearla blew across her cup. "If you don't mind me asking, where did you go just now?"

Sev considered. "I asked one of my father's friends to help me get to Terra Firma. It takes special equipment, stuff you can't get around here. Really, stuff you can't get anywhere. Unless you know where to look."

Pearla nodded, understanding on her face. "And you are worried about what your father might think?"

Sev sighed. "A little. He loves Uncle Dak, but he wouldn't want me to go alone, for sure. But I had no choice, Pearla. And Uncle Dak is harmless…just a little rough around the edges."

Pearla took a sip. "So, why did you need to go tonight?"

Sev bit her lip. "I owed him something. We struck a bargain for the goods he provided. But in the end, he didn't want payment."

"That was nice of him," Pearla remarked. "Maybe he's not that bad after all."

Sev smiled. "He isn't. And he cares for my dad, which makes him ok in my book."

A yawn interrupted her, and she stifled it with her hand. "I better turn in, Pearla. My eyes are closing already."

Pearla reached across the table and laid her hand on her arm. "Before you go, Sev, there's something you should hear." Pearla looked down, perhaps gathering courage. "Thank you for what you did for us. You're an amazing young woman…you can do things I could never dream of. And I just wanted you to know that I'm so proud to know you and to love you."

It touched Sev deeply, and she placed her hand over Pearla's, patting it fondly. "Don't stay up too late," she said.

Pearla laughed. "Mothering me, too, I see."

Sev walked away toward her room. She looked over her shoulder. "Someone has to," she said with a smile.

She readied for bed, brushing her teeth and changing into her nightclothes. She let the window up to let in the breeze, the sound of the tide rushing ashore. Tomorrow, she would go down to the beach, lounge all day. She needed a reset, and her home was a perfect place to do it.

At some point, she would have to explain her absence at school; perhaps they would let her make up her work. She tried to sleep. That thought would keep through the night, at least until tomorrow.

CHAPTER 38

Phoenix was up before everyone else. He had cleared the low table in front of the couch, and he had draft paper spread out in front of him. Phoenix wore his arm, having missed it all these days without.

He was sketching languidly with his prosthetic arm, the servos whirring with the delicate motion.

It was relaxing, meditative. The morning sun was coming in through the skylight, brightening the room in warm, supple tones.

He was planning a nursery.

Not just a nursery…another room altogether. Their little house on Dobani was small, equipped for two. When Pearla joined their family, she and Phoenix naturally shared his space.

But this new life deserved a room of its own. Sev would gladly bunk with the baby, of course, but Phoenix respected his daughter's privacy. She was 16 now, accustomed to her own space. Phoenix had little knowledge of babies, but he doubted they slept the night, especially in the beginning.

Pearla walked into the living room wrapped in a robe, her arms folded. She yawned, stifling it with her hand. "What are you up to so early?"

Phoenix looked up, his eyes bright. "Planning, Pearl. We don't have long to make this happen, so we better start now."

Pearla's mouth quirked into a smile. "And what are we making happen?"

He stood, gesturing, his arms wide. "A nursery, sweet Pearla." He walked toward her then, pressing into her space. He laid his hand against her belly. "For our precious babe."

She looked up at him, smiling, and leaned in for a kiss. He obliged her and kissed her gently. After a few moments, Pearla pulled away. "Have you had breakfast, my love?"

He hummed. "I thought we'd go out when Sev gets up. To the diner…the three of us."

Pearla grinned. "That's a lovely idea, Phoenix. I'll get us some stim, in the meantime." Her eyes fell over his shoulder to the drawing he was working on. "Want to show me?"

He nodded excitedly. "Absolutely," he said. Phoenix returned to his spot on the couch, and Pearla retrieved two cups of stim, still steaming from the pot.

Phoenix took one gratefully and gave it a sip. He sighed. "I missed this," he said. "A good cup of stim, and my best girl. This morning couldn't get better."

Pearla blushed, but hid it behind her cup. Behind them, Sev emerged from her bedroom, still in her pajamas. "Morning, you two," she mumbled. "Any stim brew left?"

Phoenix chuckled. "I remember when you used to chide me for it, and now you're hooked, too."

Sev smiled. "You must be a bad influence."

She returned to the living room and sat on the couch across from them, drawing up one of her legs beneath her. "What are you looking at?"

Pearla set her cup down. "Your father's thinking of building a nursery for the baby," Pearla said.

Sev hummed, sipping her stim, and her eyebrows lifted.

"Not thinking, Pearla, my dear, planning. I've got it all right here."

Sev smiled, something knowing in her expression. Phoenix recognized that look; it was the quiet belief in him, the same one he'd seen since she was little.

"I was thinking of knocking out this wall here and here," he began. The nursery would be beside your room, Sev."

She smiled. "I like that, Daddy. Me and my new best friend will be practical bunkmates."

It pleased Phoenix. "We'll give the baby a window here," he pointed, "plenty of natural light. She'll grow into the size just fine, and we'll change out the furniture as needed."

Pearla's eyes grew large. "What do you mean 'she', Phoenix? You don't know if this baby is a boy or girl."

Phoenix smiled. "It's a girl. Another little princess for me to spoil; I can feel it. And I've a nose for such things."

Sev looked at Pearla and gave her a meaningful smile. "Better trust it, Pearla. Dad does have good instincts."

Pearla just shook her head, smiling. "If you're wrong, you owe me an apology."

Phoenix grinned. "I'll name her myself if I'm right."

After they'd finished their stim, Phoenix loaded everyone into the transport, and they headed to their favorite diner.

They settled in the booth, and the waitress gave them their menus. The sun was high; it was mid-morning already and proved to be a beautiful day. Sev ordered her usual, but Phoenix kept suggesting things for Pearla to try. "The baby might like it," he would argue, and she would relent, predictably. It was fun to watch.

After they had ordered, Sev cleared her throat. *It was now or never.*

"Daddy, I wanted to ask you something. I meant to ask you before, but I messed up. And now it's almost too late."

He leaned in, concerned. "Out with it, mouse. Whatever it is, I'll hear you out."

She smiled. "The father/daughter dance is in a few days, Daddy. I would be honored if you would be my escort."

She blushed furiously, waiting for his answer. In retrospect, the asking was not as bad as she thought. She only wished she'd done it sooner.

Phoenix smiled, a finger to his chin. "There's nothing in this world I'd like more, little mouse, than to have you on my arm for the evening." He looked over at Pearla, and she was beaming. "I don't have long to get a suit, though."

Pearla waved her hand, a gentle smile on her face. "I'll pick you up something tomorrow. I'm going back to work."

Phoenix looked alarmed. "Don't you think you should rest, my love? The baby—"

"Will be fine, Phoenix," she finished. She laid her hand on his prosthetic arm, patting him gently. "Prescott said I can live my life as normal until near the end of my pregnancy."

Sev watched her father struggle with the information. She knew more than anything his urge to protect, to care for. How it sometimes clouded his judgement. She saw him when he finally accepted, with difficulty, that he couldn't smother her. She saw him let go of the fight before it could start.

"Of course," he said, relenting. He leaned over and kissed her cheek. "Do you have a doctor lined up here on Dobani?"

Pearla shook her head. "I thought Sev might help me look. After the dance, of course."

Sev hummed her assent. "Of course, Pearla. Anything I can do to help."

Their food arrived, and they ate heartily. Phoenix's appetite had grown voracious since he was feeling better, and Sev was glad. It did her good to see him enjoy food again. Enjoying life again.

She smiled to herself. Everything was coming together now. The new baby, Phoenix's plan for the nursery. All was as it should be.

CHAPTER 39

B y the time they got home from the diner, there were transports in the driveway. News of Phoenix's illness had spread throughout the neighborhood, and his neighbors had shown up in full force. They'd trimmed the yard neatly, swept the boardwalk and deck clean. One neighbor had a key for emergencies, and he had opened the front door and let everyone into the kitchen.

The three of them walked into the maelstrom that was their home. The kitchen smelled amazing; covered dishes sat on the counters, the kitchen table. Youngsters ran through the living room, playing tag. Phoenix watched them, smiling. Sev realized he was imagining the baby among them, perhaps remembering when she'd been that young.

A neighbor met Phoenix with his hand outstretched, and he shook it. "It's good to have you back, neighbor. You were sorely missed."

Phoenix smiled, thanking him. Sev wandered into the kitchen. Some neighbors were doing the laundry, drying and folding with a big smile on their faces. Others were cleaning where Sev had fallen short of finishing the day before. She looked around, amazed. Dobani Outskirts was a tight-knit community. Sev felt blessed to live here.

Pearla called everyone together. Some had plates of food, others had cups of cider. Neighbors lounged on couches and in chairs. The children sprawled on the living room rug.

"I want to thank everyone for what you've done for us. We love being a part of your lives, and you have certainly touched ours for the better."

Phoenix walked up to her, wrapping his arm around her waist. Sev watched from the couch, occasionally speaking to the children and answering their questions.

"We also have an announcement," Phoenix said. He tucked Pearla against him. "We're going to have a baby."

Cheers erupted in the small house. Congratulations went up from everyone. People clapped Sev on the back, asking her if she was ready to be a big sister.

"And if you would be inclined to help, I'll be starting the nursery soon. It'd go a lot faster with some extra hands."

Someone stepped forward. It was the neighbor that greeted him from before. "You can count on me, Phoenix."

Phoenix smiled. Another neighbor stepped up, and then another. Before Sev realized it, over six people had volunteered to help build the nursery.

The celebration lasted another hour, then they dispersed. Before the last neighbor left, they had washed and put away the dishes and had stored the leftovers in the fridge. Neighbors had washed and folded the laundry and tidied the house. Sev walked through the rooms, her heart full.

"Everyone is so happy to have you home, Daddy," she said to her father. He sat on the couch. He had his glasses on, reading all the news he'd missed. "And most of all, me."

He smiled at her fondly. "I'm a blessed man," he said. "There's nothing for it."

She leaned down and pecked his cheek. "I'm off to the beach, Daddy. I need some warmth to chase away the Ocarro chill. You're ok here while Pearla naps?"

He nodded. "More than, baby. Enjoy your day. Don't get too much sun, now."

She headed off to her bedroom to get ready.

◆ ◆ ◆

The days flew by. Phoenix started the demolition, and his help arrived shortly after. They had the frame up for the new room in a couple of days.

They ate the meals prepared by the neighbors and washed and returned the dishes. Pearla returned to work, and Sev to school. Life was getting back to normal.

The day of the dance had finally arrived.

Pearla twirled the iron, releasing Sev's hair into a pretty curl. They sat at the mirrored dresser in Sev's bedroom. Phoenix was working on the nursery, as usual. He still had to shower and get ready.

She wrapped another section of Sev's hair, let it set, and released it. It, too, sprang into a curl.

Sev watched her in the mirror. Pearla finished curling the rest of her hair, then tossed it with her fingers. The curls bounced along Sev's shoulders, creating body and movement. Pearla pinned the sides back with a jeweled clip.

She kissed Sev's cheek. "You're almost ready. How beautiful you look!"

Sev blushed, deepening the dusty rose she already wore on her cheeks. Pearla had helped her with her makeup; it was light and youthful, just enough to augment her eyes and coloring.

Sev placed her hand over Pearla's where it rested on her shoulder. "Thank you, Pearla. I'm not the best at girly dress-up stuff. I couldn't have done it without you."

Pearla smiled. "Want to know a secret?"

Sev nodded eagerly, her eyes sparkling. "I always wanted someone I could play dress-up with," Pearla said. "I'm an only child, you see. No playmates."

Sev laughed. "I'll be your doll any time you're in the mood, Pearla." Sev eyed her meaningfully. "Who knows? You may have another little doll to dress up soon."

Pearla sighed. "You and your father, with your assumptions. What if it's a boy?"

Sev smiled. "We can dress him up in boy's clothes," Sev reasoned. "It's the same thing."

Pearla hugged her from behind, and Sev patted her arm. "I'm glad I'm able to do this with you," she mused. "The dance, but the baby, too. Come on. Let's get you into your dress."

Pearla took it off the hanger and smoothed it with her hand. The taffeta layers gleamed in the light. "This is going to look so stunning on you, Sev. I can hardly wait."

Pearla helped her step in and zip up the back, and Sev turned to show her.

For a few moments, Pearla said nothing. Her eyes grew wet, and she pressed her hand to her chest.

"So beautiful, Sev," she said a little breathlessly. "But don't take my word for it."

Pearla turned her around to face the mirror, and Sev took in her reflection.

The dress was a deep red color, off the shoulder with a raised hem in front. Layers of gossamer taffeta silk cascaded voluminously from the natural waist. The only jewelry she wore was the little calcet bird pendant that her father had given her all those years ago, and the rosy hue picked up the tones in the dress beautifully. Her shoes, small heels the color of the dress, were the perfect complement to the ensemble.

Pearla had made her face just so, stained her lips a shade lighter than the dress, and shadowed her eyes just enough for them to sparkle. Her hair fell in delicate curls around her shoulders, pulled back on the sides, with two pieces coming down to frame her face. She felt very unlike herself, but very grown up. She felt pretty, and she was not used to seeing herself that way.

"See?" Pearla told her, standing behind and looking at her reflection with her. "Most beautiful girl I've ever seen."

Sev ducked her head, unused to such flattery. She looked up and her eyes glittered with tears. "Do you think Dad will like it?"

Pearla smiled. "Oh, he absolutely will, Sev. Just you wait and see."

She sat her down at the dresser. "Speaking of, I've got to go light a fire under him…he'll work on that nursery until it's time to go. I'll be back. Don't come out until he's ready! It will spoil the surprise."

She left her there, alone with her thoughts. As time wore on, she grew more and more nervous.

Sev was about ready to shake out of her shoes when a tentative knock came at the door. The knob twisted, and it was Pearla.

"Your father's ready, Pearla. He looks so handsome! Come out when you can. You'll need to leave soon if you're going to make the dance."

She left, and Sev blew out a breath. A few moments later, Sev opened the door to her room and walked out into the living room.

Her father was standing there in a new suit and tie. He was wearing his arm and had his hands crossed in front of him. He had swept his hair back; it was not heavily styled, but it lay enough away from his forehead that she could see he'd put effort into his appearance. It reminded her of her adoption, all those years ago, and how he'd dressed up for that, too.

Her throat tightened, and she thought she might cry. She didn't. She gave him a shy smile, nervously pressing the taffeta of her dress.

Phoenix said nothing for several moments, apparently stunned. "Stars alive, little mouse. When did you grow up on me?"

Sev smiled. Pearla watched the two, a big grin on her face.

"You look as beautiful and as rare as anything I might dream of," Phoenix told her. "I'm an honored man tonight, to be sure."

Pearla withdrew her holopad and held it up. "A hologram," she said. "And don't fuss, Phoenix. You're taking one, like it or not."

He grinned and feigned annoyance. He posed with Sev in front of the fireplace, her arm threaded through his.

Pearla took all the pictures she wanted, then ushered them out the door. "You two better get going," she said. "You might be late as it is."

They said their goodbyes, and she and her father made their way to the transport.

The two of them traveled in silence. Phoenix drove. The stars came out one by one. The night was clear and beautiful.

By the time they got to the school, Sev was nervous again. Dancing in front of her friends was a terrifying prospect; she hadn't thought about that when she asked Phoenix to go with her. Maybe she should've skipped the dance altogether.

Phoenix's warm hand on hers quieted her thoughts. He'd opened the door for her while she was spiraling with doubt and was now offering to help her out of the transport.

She looked up at him, matching his smile. She stood, and he offered her his arm.

"Don't ask where a rogue like me learned to be a gentleman," he said wryly. "Must be all of those holographs you watch rubbing off on me."

Sev laughed, and it dispelled her nerves some. He opened the door for her, and they walked into the gymnasium.

The students had draped the ceiling, and fairy lights hung down around them. Columns with vines and leafy backdrops twined around the dance floor. Photo ops stood at every corner, but Sev had taken enough of those at home.

A quartet played beautiful music, and Phoenix led her to the dance floor.

Sev resisted, looking down at her feet. Her stomach twisted. The other couples glided effortlessly across the dance floor. She clenched her dress in her hands. She was going to make a fool of herself.

"What's the matter, mouse?" her father asked softly. "Want to eat first?"

She shook her head. "I don't know how to dance, Daddy. I should've told you."

He chuckled. "Don't fret it, sweet mouse." He clasped her hand in his and wrapped his other arm around her. "Follow my lead. I know a thing or two."

She smiled. What couldn't he do? she marveled. He never ceased to amaze her; his unpredictability was one thing she always loved about him.

"I step back, you step forward," he whispered. "You won't step on my toes, and if you do, you won't hurt me. Ok? On the beat."

Phoenix stepped back, and she stepped forward. She followed his lead. It was easier than she thought it would be. She was soon relaxed and enjoying herself.

"You've got natural rhythm, Sev," he told her. "Unlike your dad here. I have to work at it."

She laughed. "There's very little you have to work at, Daddy," she told him. He twirled them, and she grew lightheaded for a moment. She looked up at him. The fairy lights augmented his white patch and the intermittent gray in his hair, making him look dashing. She grew strangely sentimental, and her mouth turned down.

"Thank you for raising me," she said. "I never thanked you for it. You changed your life because of me."

Phoenix blinked back tears. "No, Sev. *You* changed my life. You saved me from myself. I'm a different man now, because of you."

She smiled, her heart filled to overflowing. She rested her head against her father's shoulder and let him lead them through the dance. It was the way he had always led them. The way they'd lead each other through whatever life had thrown their way. It was just them. Then Pearla. Now, the baby.

She looked up at him. "I'm happy about the baby, Daddy. Truly I am. I didn't want you to think otherwise."

He tightened his arm around her. "I know, sweetheart. I'll love this baby too, but you'll always be my little girl."

She nodded. They danced the rest of the evening and left under a flawless night sky. They arrived home well after the tide had come in.

Pearla was on the couch, asleep, a holopad in her lap. Phoenix scooped her up gingerly and carried her into their bedroom. When he returned, Sev had already kicked off her shoes. She was leaning back on the couch and staring up at the skylight, her feet propped on the low table. The stars shone vividly through the glass.

He crossed to her and kissed the top of her head. "You're a lovely dancer, sweet mouse. You have a good night now. Your old man is beat."

She bid him a good night and watched him walk back into his bedroom. She sat there for a long time, still in her dress, thinking. The night had been perfect, but change was coming. She could feel it.

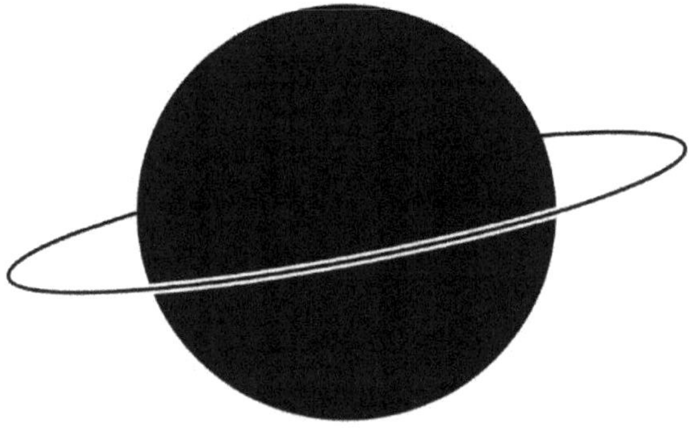

CHAPTER 40

Phoenix finished the nursery on a Sunday. Once they'd framed the room, he'd shut it off to everyone but the neighbors who had volunteered to help, hoping to keep it a surprise as long as possible.

The night before, Sev won first prize at the Science Fair for her successful experiment, and they all went out to eat at the diner to celebrate.

Pearla had a little belly now. She could still wear her clothes, but if you were really paying attention, you could tell she was pregnant. She was pleased and would preen in front of the mirror while getting dressed. "Imagine when I get really huge, Sev. What a sight that will be!"

Phoenix gathered them all for the big reveal. Sev held a holopad, hoping to take some pictures to show to her friends. With a comical drumroll, he opened the door, and they stepped inside.

The room was a muted, pale yellow, the color of a Dobani sunrise. A beautiful white crib stood by the new window, intricately carved. A large, comfortable chair sat in the corner. Phoenix sat down it, demonstrating how it would rock back and forth.

But Sev's favorite part was the stars on the ceiling.

The ceiling was painted black; nebulae and galaxies exploded in bright, beautiful reds, purples, and blues. Specks of white stars dotted the night's canvas. The baby could lie in bed and dream of the stars, could imagine itself among them. It was a beautiful thought.

On the matching white dresser stood a model of the skiff. It was perfect to scale and detail, down to the blue hull. Sev pointed her holopad at the model and took a picture.

Pearla exhaled. "Oh Phoenix," she breathed. "I never imagined it would be so—"

"Perfect," Sev finished. "It's perfect, Daddy. You did such an amazing job."

Pearla went over to where Phoenix sat in the chair and stood by him. "I want you to name the baby, Phoenix. Boy or girl."

Phoenix beamed. "Boy or girl," he said, thinking. He closed his eyes, resting his head against the chair. After a moment, he looked up at Pearla, then Sev. "Lorien," he whispered. "If that's ok with you two."

Sev's eyes grew wide. Her father had mentioned her Uncle Lorien in passing. She wished she could've met him. She smiled then, her eyes welling with tears. "I think it's the perfect name, Daddy."

Pearla laid a hand on his shoulder. "I agree." She pressed her hand to the gentle swell of her belly. "What do you think, Lori? You like your name? Hmm? You like that, little Lorien?"

Sev laughed. Her father was grinning, beyond happy, and clasped Pearla's hand.

Sev excused herself. She returned with her pack. "I have a present," she said. "For Lorien."

She opened her pack and withdrew the blue calcet.

Her father gasped. "As I live and breathe," he muttered.

Sev walked over to the crib, hesitating for just a moment. This piece of calcet meant something special to the Verdani, and it had traveled with her through some of the hardest trials of her life. Now, it would belong to someone new.

She laid it on a blanket printed with stars.

Phoenix and Pearla walked over to where Sev stood, looking into the crib. The calcet suddenly glowed, pulsing like a heartbeat.

"It's so beautiful, Sev," Pearla said.

Phoenix nodded. "A jewel for a jewel." He reached for Sev's hand. "Thank you, little mouse. For everything."

She smiled. They stood there watching it for a long time after.

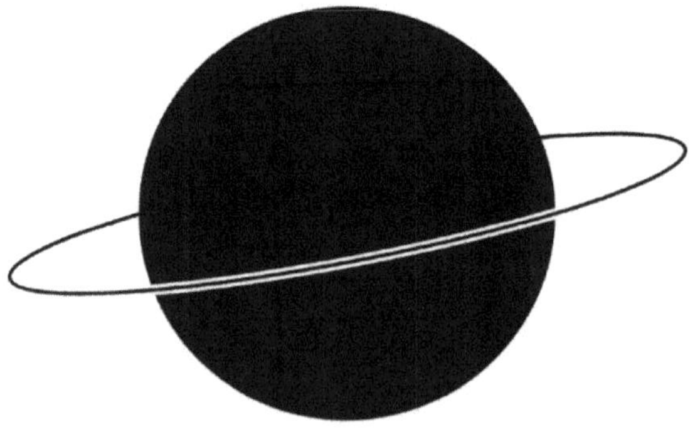

About the Author

Jessahme Wren is an award-winning author of evocative short fiction, poetry, and novels. With a passion for storytelling, she crafts works that explore the depth of human emotion and the complexities of life. She lives in the scenic heart of Southwest Alabama, where the natural world and the people around her provide endless inspiration. When she's not writing, she enjoys spending time with her family and pets, as well as discovering new places through travel. *Terra Nova* is her third book.

Keep up to date on news and all my books here:

Thank you for purchasing this book.
If you enjoyed your read, please provide feedback in the
form of a review.

www.ingramcontent.com/pod-product-compliance
Lightning Source LLC
Chambersburg PA
CBHW061100100726
47911CB00012B/317